When Shakespeare Lost the Plot

When Shakespeare Lost the Plot

An outlandish play, staged in India, makes the Bard stand on his head, gives Hamlet a happy ending and destroys Western philosophy.

Anand Subhuti

First published in India in 2015 by CinnamonTeal Publishing

Copyright © 2015 Anand Subhuti

ISBN 978-93-85523-09-0

Swami Anand Subhuti asserts the moral right to be identified as the author of this work. All rights reserved. No part of this publication may be produced, stored in a retrieval system, or transmitted in any form or by any means without the prior written permission of the author, nor be otherwise circulated in any form of binding or cover other than that in which it is published and without a similar condition being imposed on the subsequent purchaser.

Play: When Shakespeare Lost the Plot © 2011 Swami Anand Subhuti. All rights reserved.

Typesetting and cover design: CinnamonTeal Publishing, Goa, India.

Author's website: www.anandsubhuti.com

CinnamonTeal Publishing
an imprint of Dogears Print Media Pvt. Ltd.
Plot No 16, Housing Board Colony
Gogol, Margao
Goa 403601 India
www.cinnamonteal.in

Acknowledgments

This is a book about staging an unusual play, which was performed three times, twice in India and once in Europe. On each occasion it was anchored by a talented actress playing the key role of Mrs Shakespeare. So, first of all, I'd like to pay tribute to these three women:

Salila, who rescued the first, hastily-produced version at Nehru Hall in Pune.

Anasha, who raised the bar for all of us with her excellent performance at the Ishanya Amphitheatre in Pune.

Ashika, who gave a heart-warming rendition of the Bard's wife at the Osho Risk Summer Festival in Denmark.

Thank you, each one of you, for helping me convey the spirit of the play. Much gratitude to all those who acted in the three productions, or helped in some way, and especially to Ragni, my co-producer in India, who made it all possible.

A big thank you to Sheelu, my main sponsor, who has generously supported several projects of mine in various ways, and also to Ida, who added her support for the Ishanya production.

Thanks also to all my friends at the Osho Resort in Pune and the Risk Institute in Denmark. These two energy fields have provided sources of personal nourishment for me from which I could venture forth with my creative productions.

Contents

But this I say, no hesitation,

Will never knew of meditation.

His busy mind was full of chatter

He didn't think the silence mattered.

~ Prologue

Introduction

To be or not to be...?

Sooner or later, someone had to answer the question. It's kinda surprising that the answer, when it came, was the exact opposite of what everyone expected.

~ Anand Subhuti

Chapter One

Frying Eggs for Hamlet

*H*amlet answered the door in his underwear – in a pair of boxer shorts, to be precise. Besides which, he wore a sheepish grin and nothing else. Until I rang the doorbell, he was sleeping. Ophelia, I guessed, was still in bed and gently yawning, stretching her sweet young body under the covers, stealing a few more minutes, not quite ready to face the bright sunshine in their living room.

These two were night owls...party people. If it wasn't for our appointment, rashly made for ten o'clock, they probably wouldn't surface until around eleven, or even noon. Yesterday, for example, they were talking with friends about arranging an all-night, slumber-style 'pyjama party', which challenges my imagination because neither of them wear pyjamas.

"Hi," said Hamlet, then led me into the kitchen.

"Coffee?" he inquired.

I nodded. He put on the kettle and took three dirty cups out of a pile of dishes in the sink, washed them and reached for the large Nescafe jar on the counter.

"If you wanna make fried eggs, I'd appreciate it."

That sounded reasonable. I'd eaten a bowl of porridge two hours earlier and was peckish. I lit the gas ring, took a box of eggs from the fridge, cracked them and started frying. Hamlet made coffee for three, pushed one cup towards me and took the other two out onto the patio. It was already warm out there. Nights can be cold in India, in the beginning of December, but as soon as the sun comes up the temperature soars to a comfortable 25 degrees Celsius.

Hamlet sank heavily into a plain white plastic chair, reached for a pack of tobacco on the little table in front of him and began rolling a cigarette. Pretty soon, Ophelia appeared, a friendly but ghostly apparition from the bedroom, wearing only an elegantly ripped t-shirt. Her blonde hair was a delightful mess and her bare, slim legs were nicely bronzed from a recent trip to the beaches of Goa.

Peering in my direction through half-closed eyes, she nodded a silent 'good morning' and wandered sleepily across the living room, out onto the patio, sat down beside Hamlet, took a sip of coffee and rolled her own cigarette.

When the toast and eggs were ready, I gave them both a plate, then sat down next to them. Nobody spoke. It was clear that both Hamlet and Ophelia needed their morning shots of nicotine, caffeine and protein before joining the world of the awakened.

Hamlet knew what I was thinking. I could tell from the way he didn't look at me; just kept studying his plate with an amused, unfocused stare. He knew what I'd come to hear. Still, he had to finish his eggs, take another sip of coffee and stub out the burning butt of his cigarette before making eye contact. When he did, his face lit up with a mischievous smile.

　　　Anand Subhuti

"We've decided we're not going to work in the Resort this year," he informed me.

I laughed in surprise, delighted at the news, and pretty soon Hamlet and Ophelia were laughing with me. They knew how much these words meant to me.

These were the words that opened the door. They completed my casting and made the play possible. They gave me the green light to go ahead and rent the most expensive theatre in the City of Pune and put on a play that would lose several thousand dollars of my personal money. But I didn't care. It was worth it.

Like me, Hamlet and Ophelia were in the habit of coming to India every year to meditate, work, or simply hang out at the Osho Meditation Resort in Pune. Like me, they were willing to give the Resort a miss for a few weeks in order to tread the boards of dramatic romance.

Hamlet was Korean-American, born in Seoul and raised in Los Angeles. He was 40 years old with a flat, moon-like face and long black hair that made him look like a cross between Jackie Chan, Bruce Lee and an Apache warrior.

If you're thinking "Hmm, not your typical Prince of Denmark," I can only agree. But he was good looking, brimming over with youthful energy and had great stage presence even though he was only a beginner at acting. Wait, let me qualify that: he used to be a City of London banker, which, according to my cynical view of global finance, definitely requires acting skills – after all, you have to convince the public you're trustworthy.

But Hamlet gained my trust in a different way. He flipped the bird to mainstream values, left the City and took off for the Mystic East, seeking deeper answers to life than brokering hedge funds and selling snake oil.

In India, he met Ophelia, a sexy, 25-year-old German art student with tattoos on her body, a ring through her lower lip and a sense of adventure that made her impulsively jump on the back of Hamlet's motorbike and drive off into the sunset with him.

One year previously, before they came on board my project, they had been living and working in the Osho Resort, one of the subcontinent's more classy meditation destinations. Set within Pune's only green suburb and therefore insulated from the traffic, pollution and general madness of your typical Indian city, the Resort offered a wide range of meditation and entertainment, catering to an international clientele.

Hamlet was the driving force behind the Events Team, which had the task of staging nightly diversions for the Resort visitors', ranging from black-and-white disco parties to *Meditators Got Talent* variety shows. If you're wondering why an Indian ashram would wish to combine introverted meditation with extroverted night life, I might be able to come up with an explanation, but right now it would take too long. Maybe it will become clear as we progress.

Anyway, Hamlet was their man of the moment, bursting with creative ideas. He loved nothing better than to pick up a microphone in front of a crowd and say "Good evening, everyone..." And, of course, as an American, he was genetically disposed towards showbiz. The Resort managers loved him and wanted him back for another season, but the appeal of my theatre project won out. He was hooked on Ham.

Ophelia, his girlfriend, adored the idea of playing the famous role and I adored her, because she already looked the part. Admittedly, in daily life, she seemed far too happy, but otherwise her pale skin, blood-red lips and blonde tresses would all look terrific under moody stage lighting. Add a long white diaphanous gown and a mournful expression and there you have your classic, doomed, despairing, youthful tragedienne.

It was, in short, a package deal, an extension of a real-life love affair, a theatrical marriage not exactly made in heaven – neither of these two was going win an Academy Award – but good enough for me to declare "Yes, this show is going to happen!"

The other four major acting roles were already filled, so maybe this is a good moment to introduce them:

The Bard himself. Well, that was me. I decided to play the part of William Shakespeare. At 67 years of age, bald and bearded, English and intellectual, I could just get away with it, although I have to admit that my grey beard made me look older than the only known portrait of the Bard – the rakish-looking fellow, sporting a gold ring in his left ear, who gazes out of the Chandos painting. Not surprising, really, because Will died at the age of 52.

This may seem premature to us, but when you learn how many times the Elizabethan theatres in London had to shut down because of plague epidemics sweeping through the city, it's a miracle he lived that long.

Plague was rampant at the end of the 16th century and the Globe and other theatres were ideal places for catching it. The whole country suffered but London, fittingly enough, was deemed to be the plague capital, so much so that on one occasion Queen Elizabeth I fled to Windsor, erected a gallows and declared anyone coming from London should be hanged.

The Bard, we assume, remained in the capital, even

when the theatres were closed, but nevertheless survived long enough to write 38 plays and 154 sonnets. He retired at the age of 49 to Stratford-upon-Avon and soon thereafter expired. He may have died of the plague – nobody really knows.

It's strange that I wrote a play about Shakespeare because I hated him with a passion when I was at school. I guess all the kids of my generation did; well, anyway, the middle-class kids who went to 'academic' schools and were force-fed Shakespeare's plays in dusty classrooms on sunny days, when we all should have been chilling at the beach.

But then, I have to grudgingly concede that Shakespeare saved my life. I'll come to it later.

So, I was holding down the Bard's role. Meanwhile, three more friends had expressed enthusiasm for the parts of Queen Elizabeth Ist, Mrs Shakespeare and Nobody.

The role of Good Queen Bess was taken by a long-time friend of mine. She was born to play it. In her mid-60s and raised in Hampstead, London, she uttered the Queen's English with an impeccable upper-middle-class accent, exuding an effortlessly superior demeanour and was therefore a shoo-in for the role.

Don't get me wrong. In real life, Her Majesty was a gentle soul, a caring and generous friend to me and something of an emotional anchor in times of instability, chaos and stress – which tended to happen to me fairly frequently, due to my insecure lifestyle as a spiritual gypsy.

But like I said, she was a class act. I don't think she ever thought of herself as superior to anyone, but that's how she came across. I remember one time: Over lunch one day in the Resort's canteen, a group of us were discussing

                    Anand Subhuti

how difficult it was to arrange to shift some furniture from one house to another in Koregaon Park – the Pune suburb where we all lived.

Her Royal Highness looked at us in a puzzled way and enquired, with the genuine innocence of the aristocracy, "Can't the *ayahs* do it?"

Of course, we all cracked up laughing.

In fairness, though, I have to say that we all had *ayahs* – our favourite term, borrowed from the days of the British Raj, for female Indian servants. They were cheap, readily available, spoke pidgin English and were eager to work for Westerners, whom they could manipulate and cheat far more easily than their local, mean-and-wealthy Indian employers.

Even Left-wing German socialists hired *ayahs* when they came to Pune, if only because long-term foreign residents like me branded them as mentally retarded if they did their own house cleaning and laundry.

No, it was the way Elizabeth said it that tickled me – that, plus the comical image of our fat, lazy *ayahs*, struggling in their saris to carry a chest of drawers across Koregaon Park.

During the past six months, my poor Queen had been suffering severely from rheumatoid arthritis, something I wouldn't wish on anyone, but it's an ill wind that blows nobody any good and her gaunt face and pained expression, combined with a limping gait, was perfect for the part of an aging, bitter old monarch determined to impose her bad mood on her luckless subjects.

Like me, Queen Bess had spent many years in Pune. We'd both arrived here in the 70s, drawn by the charismatic pull of a controversial Indian mystic, Osho, then known by the longer title of Bhagwan Shree Rajneesh.

We both joined his ashram. We both explored his vision of sex, love and meditation, although not necessarily in the same bed. We both stayed on after he died in 1990.

Ten years later, at the turn of the century, I became a global commuter, choosing to spend my summers in Europe and my winters in India. But Elizabeth settled in Pune. She found herself a cosy apartment and a cat, then spent her days collecting and publishing personal stories from people like me about life with Osho. She no longer worked in the ashram – which by this time had completed its slow mutation into a resort – and was therefore free to indulge my desire to make her Queen.

Now, for the key role in the play, the part of my dear wife:

Mrs Shakespeare was easily my most important character – even more so than the Bard himself. According to my personalized view of Elizabethan court politics, Will was basically an ass-kisser, weaselling his way into the favour of Queen Elizabeth and trying hard to convince her that it was a good idea *not* to chop off his head. In my play, he retained his precious image as a genius wordsmith, but he didn't have much backbone.

His wife, however, was the 'wise woman' personified. She was the voice of truth itself and a catalyst for the transformation the other characters would go through. Fortunately, she was also my trump card, because somehow I managed to persuade an excellent Swedish actress to take on the part.

We'd met a couple of years earlier at a seaside café in Greece, on the island of Lesbos, where we sprawled on a pair of large bean bags on a wooden deck that jutted out over the beach, talking about theatre. I liked her

     Anand Subhuti

hypnotic blue eyes, pale skin, dark brown hair and the deepening sense of intimacy that grew between us as the morning progressed.

We almost fell in love, but somehow didn't, and so became friends. Later, I learned she was coming to India and, without holding out much hope, sent her a copy of the script and an invitation to join my acting team. To my delight, she accepted.

Mrs Shakespeare was 37 years old and earned her bread and butter by performing in a Swedish pop group that imitated Abba. When she said 'yes' to my request, I sighed in relief, because I knew she would anchor my play. I knew, now, that it would work.

Finally, we come to the joker in the pack, the part of Nobody. Nobody was a time-warp character who gave the play its mystical dimension. He was a bit like Doctor Who, a bit like Merlin the Magician, and a whole lot like the characters whom Alice meets when she climbs *Through the Looking Glass*.

It was Nobody who was able to solve the dilemma posed by the Bard's most famous line: *To be or not to be*. It was Nobody who allowed me to dispose of it, once and for all. It was he who took us deep into the human psyche – far deeper than Will Shakespeare ever ventured – and revealed the existential truth of 'not to be'. In short, it was he who destroyed Western philosophy, supplanting it with Eastern mysticism.

This, basically, is why I decided to write a book about this play, because the implications are enormous, far bigger than my poor talent as a writer can hope to demonstrate – and yet I have to try. At the very least, I have to hint at the awful poverty in which we Westerners have been living, a poverty far greater than that to be found in India – a poverty of the soul.

I notice I've been referring to Nobody as 'he' but the part was androgynous. It could be played by a man or a woman and, indeed, for this quirky role, I invited a young Indian woman who was, in my eyes, a powerhouse of energy, a human dynamo, always on the go, obsessed with being active and productive.

For years, Nobody worked in the resort canteen – for so long, in fact, that when I close my eyes I can still see her scraping vegetarian lasagne off the serving trays. She had a thick mop of black hair, a pretty face and a wide mouth that could either give you a brilliant smile or suddenly utter unpalatable and inconvenient truths. Tact wasn't her strong suit.

Nobody also possessed a short, stocky body which refused to shrink with dieting. When, in despair, she wrote to Osho about her weight issue, he replied, "Don't go on a diet, fall in love." She did and it worked. She got together with a German guy, moved with him to Deutschland and lost kilos.

I have never met anyone so busy. Even when she left the canteen and trained in Cranio-Sacral Healing, Nobody was always volunteering as a helper in long trainings, shifting massage tables around, setting up group rooms. But she had a soft spot for theatre and had danced and acted her way through several musicals I'd written and produced in the 90s. After checking her schedule, agreed to play the part.

By the way, nobody got paid. Umm... well... I don't mean that Nobody was the only one who got paid and the rest of us did not. I mean, we all did the show for free, out of enthusiasm.

          Anand Subhuti

By now, surely, you will have noticed the cosmopolitan nature of our cast: two actors from England, one from Germany, one from Korea-America, one from Sweden, and one from India. Not your average Shakespearian troupe.

We got to know each other in Pune, over the years, because we were *sannyasins*, as disciples of Osho were called. That's how we happened to be there, in December 2013, when I passed around my script and invited them to make my thespian dream come true.

They all said 'yes' and with Hamlet and Ophelia climbing aboard, the project was ready to roll. Pretty soon, the living room of their apartment would become our main rehearsal space. Arriving early and frying eggs would be my daily task in order to get Hamlet and Ophelia out of bed and ready to work by the time the others came.

Mrs Shakespeare, Queen Elizabeth and Nobody, would arrive on bicycles from various parts of Koregaon Park, looking fresh, energized and ready to rehearse. No need to wake them up. Mrs Shakespeare and Nobody made the journey from the southern side of the park, which traffic-wise was quiet. But the Queen, in spite of her advancing years and arthritis, braved the intense and chaotic rush hour on North Main Road, the main traffic artery through this part of town, which, in my estimation, earned her a gold star for courage.

I'd started bicycling in Koregaon Park, years ago, for health reasons – to keep fit. I gave it up for a similar reason – to stay in one piece. The traffic got so crazy I knew, sooner or later, I'd get flattened. Indeed, I even heard a rumour that trainee surgeons from around India came to Pune hospitals to practice their skills, because there are more traffic accidents here than anywhere else. It didn't surprise me.

But the Queen... the Queen rode on, defying some of the worst drivers ever to be found on four wheels. Perhaps the very sight of her intimidated them, for her lower face was hidden behind a large air filtration mask, her eyes behind a pair of dark glasses and her hair under a huge floppy cap. With this tall, alien-looking creature bearing down on you, it's understandable you might suddenly swerve to let her pass unharmed.

However, at that particular moment, before rehearsals began, it was just Hamlet, Ophelia and me in the apartment. It was a moment to relax, enjoy my casting success and catch my breath before the long pilgrimage to showtime began.

Watching the two of them, sitting in casual intimacy on the patio, I was struck by the fact that normal life rarely, if ever, gets onstage. Entertainment, by definition, is created by drama, and drama by the unusual, the unfortunate... and the tragic.

Look at it this way: let's suppose, for a moment, that Hamlet's uncle didn't kill his father. I'd like to refer to his father by name, but it seems that ghosts don't have names, so we never get to know what Hamlet's father was actually called.

Nowadays, of course, he could be called anything, due to international, cross-cultural fertilization. For example, I'm told that the most common name for baby boys in Denmark today is 'William', which I strongly suspect is due to the popularity of the British monarchy and the recent wedding of Prince William to Kate Middleton.

But in those bygone Elizabethan days, a Danish king would have been called Frederik, Christian, Rasmus, Andreas, Cnut...

 Anand Subhuti

I'm partial to Cnut. That was the name of the only Dane I ever learned about in my high school history lessons, although my teachers Anglicized it into 'Canute'.

Back in the early 11th century, after invading England and slaughtering an impressive number of Anglo-Saxon kings, Cnut the Dane became a most pious and humble monarch. So much so that, on one famous occasion – and this is the reason why he elbowed his way into our history books – Cnut placed his throne before the waves at the English seaside and ordered the incoming tide not to wet his shoes and garments.

No, apparently, he wasn't 'cnuts'. Rather, the king was exposing and ridiculing the empty flattery of his own courtiers. As the waves soaked his socks, Cnut declared "Let all men know how empty and worthless is the power of kings, for there is none worthy of the name, but He whom heaven, earth, and sea obey by eternal laws."

Cnut then hung his gold crown over a statue of Jesus nailed to the cross and vowed never to wear it again, which makes we wonder why he bothered to invade England and slaughter all those Anglo-Saxon kings in the first place. School history books never answer the interesting questions, do they?

Anyway, back to Hamlet. Let's imagine his father is alive, well and still married to Queen Gertrude. Meanwhile, Uncle Claudius, instead of pouring poison into his brother's ear, is off hunting, riding with his hounds, chasing and killing deer instead of family members.

Now picture this peaceful scene: Hamlet sitting on a patio, somewhere in Elsinore Castle, enjoying breakfast with his beloved Ophelia, just like this young couple I'm watching now. They would have to be married, of course, since medieval protocol would forbid such a casual and intimate breakfast-for-two scenario for a pair of unweds. And for sure – married or unmarried – they'd be wearing more clothes than my friends. It's not just a question of the conservative manners of their time. It's the rotten state of Denmark, or, to be more precise, the rotten state of Danish weather. You cannot have breakfast outdoors in Denmark in your underwear. I guarantee, if you do, you'll freeze your ass off. Trust me. I know what I'm talking about.

For the past ten years, I've travelled my own personal migration route between Europe and Asia, winging my way from Europe to India in the autumn, staying over the winter months, then heading back to Europe in the Spring. Residing in India over the winter guaranteed me 4-5 months of perpetual sunshine, with cool nights and warm days. Departing in the Spring meant that I avoided India's hot season, when temperatures rose above an unbearable 40 degrees Celsius, and, after the hot season came the monsoon – the long Indian wet season – when continuous humidity eventually turned my curtains, towels, mattresses, quilts and pillow cases into mould factories. I swear, you could have started a mushroom farm on my doormat.

My migration pattern also meant I avoided the European winter and arrived just in time to enjoy the summer, so it was a perfect global commute. Oh, but there was – and still is – a Catch 22. You see, the Danish calendar may tell you it's summer... June, July, August... but the weather will insist that it's not. Quite often, summer doesn't happen in Denmark. Not at all.

The natives may be hearing rumours of heatwaves in Southern Germany, balmy temperatures on the South Coast of England and sunny days in Stockholm. They

     Anand Subhuti

may, in short, be surrounded by good meteorological news, but in Hamlet's land they will be shivering as they walk through large puddles of water on the streets, straining to make progress against an unforgiving wind that moans and sighs through town and countryside alike.

"Last year, summer happened one Thursday afternoon in June," joked a Danish friend of mine, neatly summarizing the brevity of the event.

Global warming, in its rush northwards to melt the polar ice cap, seems to have leap-frogged over Denmark. So, you can be sure of one thing: Hamlet and Ophelia would be wearing a lot more than boxer shorts and t-shirts if they ventured outdoors for breakfast at Elsinore Castle.

But on that sunny January morning on the Indian subcontinent, nested comfortably between the Equator and the Tropic of Cancer, it was a different story. My friends could lounge in the skimpiest clothing, drinking their coffee, puffing on their cigarettes, content to be wordless in each other's company, sharing a space of uneventful, ordinary togetherness.

That's why I say entertainment demands drama. You can't sit onstage and do this, even if you are the Prince of Denmark and the Danish Prime Minister's daughter, and then expect the audience to give you a standing ovation.

It is true that Andy Warhol, in his quest to make art out of banality, or banality out of art, came close to succeeding when, in 1963, he created a five-and-a-half-hour movie of a guy stacking zzzzzs. It was called, appropriately enough, *Sleep*.

"It wasn't the movie that made the night for me," said one friend who sat through it. "It was the reaction in the cinema when he woke. We all stood up and cheered like crazy – that was the pay off."

Warhol's exception proved the rule. Hamlet and Ophelia could not have enjoyed their cosy togetherness onstage for long. Even if Uncle Claudius had suppressed his sibling rivalry and kept his poisonous potion away from royal ears, something out of the ordinary would *have* to happen:

🍀 The Prince of Norway arrives unannounced at Elsinore Castle and declares that Ophelia has been betrothed to him, not to Hamlet, through a forgotten pledge between the Danish and Norwegian royal families...

🍀 Ophelia's younger sister is jealous and seduces Hamlet one night during a thunderstorm, when he can't tell the difference, until suddenly Ophelia appears and he realizes his error, too late...

🍀 Hamlet's mother murders Ophelia because she is not of royal blood and therefore not good enough for her wonderful son...

I'm sure you get the point. Entertainment demands extraordinary occurrences and this, in turn, means that sooner or later the characters are going to find themselves struggling through scenes of conflict, intrigue, violence and death.

The basic dynamic of almost every tale, whether told in a play, book, movie, or TV series, is neatly enshrined in the concept 'conflict resolution': set up a conflict early in the story line, then keep your audience on the edge of their seats, preoccupied with the question 'will it all turn out okay in the end?'

Will we find out who shot JR in the TV series *Dallas?*

     Anand Subhuti

Will Marshal Gary Cooper outgun the bad guys in *High Noon?* Will Frodo make it to Mount Doom and destroy Sauron the Necromancer? Will amateur magician Harry Potter kill Voldemort, or vice versa?

Psychologists in America and Europe routinely publish social research studies showing that when children are exposed to violence through TV, movies and video games, as teenagers they are likely to be more aggressive and less sensitive to the pain and suffering of others. In other words, the line between who shot JR, who shot JFK and who shot the next-door neighbour's cat tends to get a little blurry.

These findings don't make a scrap of difference. Nothing is going to change. As long as human beings need entertainment, they are going to want something with higher adrenalin voltage than the sight of a boyfriend and girlfriend sitting cosily together, sipping coffee, eating fried eggs, gently awakening to the day.

These two will need to struggle, risking defeat, despair and, indeed, death itself, so that my play can entertain people.

Will it turn out okay? Sorry, you'll have to wait. See next gripping episode.

Chapter Two

The Mark of Greatness

Normally, I don't like Prologues. I find them boring. They insinuate themselves between the audience and the plot, delaying the action and sometimes I almost find myself standing up and shouting "Cut the crap! Get on with it!"

But when it came to directing my own play I really had no choice. Somehow, I was having visions of an Englishman with a great baritone voice walking out onto the stage in a pair of puffy, Tudor-style breeches and leg-hugging tights, unrolling his scroll and introducing my play.

Sure enough, that's what happened. You see, I needed two 'extras' in my play to be the Queen's attendants, to perform various practical functions onstage such as shifting props around, and also to join in the action, which included an up-tempo backing routine in support of a dancing Ophelia – no, really, I mean it.

As soon as they volunteered I realized one of them would make a superb Prologue. He had the stature, the voice, the presence, the BBC newscaster accent. He radiated the sheer Englishness the task required. When he opened

 Anand Subhuti

his mouth, I had no choice but to bow to destiny. Indeed, I had only to look at him and rhyming couplets started proliferating in my head.

He was in his 50s... tall, bald, clean shaven and in appearance not totally dissimilar to Patrick Stewart playing Captain Jean-Luc Picard in *Star Trek: The Next Generation*, or, at a stretch, Mr Spock, in the original series, without hair.

I didn't know him well, but enough to remember he'd been around the Resort for a good number of years and was something of a loner. He tended to be hidden away in air-conditioned offices, editing translations of Osho's discourses and I don't recall ever seeing him at a disco party. For this reason, I was surprised at his willingness to join the action; surprised and pleased.

And lo, it came to pass: at the appointed hour of the appointed day, the Prologue walked out onto my recently-rented and ruinously expensive stage, unrolled his scroll, and addressed the audience thus:

> *The mark of greatness as we know*
> *Is left for history to bestow.*
> *And who of us, now sitting here,*
> *Will be remembered through the years?*

One thing I learned from the Bard: use the Prologue to engage the audience by addressing them directly. Get them involved. So here is the first hook for Joe Public: everyone wants to be famous, recognized in one way or another, leaving a mark on history. What did Steve Jobs say?

"We're here to make a dent in the universe."

Personally, I disagree with Jobs. As far as I can tell, we're not here to dent the universe. We're here to dance with it.

But Jobs' statement reflects a common human ambition: to make a difference and to be recognized for it.

Who of us will achieve it? You... me... the guy next door? Brain food for my audience to chew on. Which brings us, speedily enough, to the man who, in literary terms, made the biggest dent of all:

> *William Shakespeare. There's a name,*
> *Four hundred years of global fame,*
> *His plays show man in good, in badness,*
> *Our vanity, our pride, our madness,*
> *The rise and fall of kings and queens,*
> *Blind ambition, broken dreams.*
> *Shakespeare's mighty pen described it,*
> *What unkind critic will deny it?*

The point I make in the first half of the prologue is hardly original: Shakespeare was a genius, poetically portraying the heights and depths of human nature. That done, I offer a slightly different take on the Bard:

> *But this I say, no hesitation,*
> *Will never knew of meditation.*
> *His busy mind was full of chatter*
> *He didn't think the silence mattered.*
> *His characters did everything*
> *But close their eyes and look within...*

True enough, wouldn't you say? For all the millions of lectures delivered in British schools and universities on the subject of William Shakespeare, I may be the first person to point out the lack of meditative awareness in the Bard's plays. Hardly surprising, really, because meditation has never been part of Western culture, which is why some

   Anand Subhuti

people in India take the view that the West has never known culture at all. After all, they argue, how can you know culture if you don't even know yourself?

Hmmm...

Anyway, this is the main thrust of my story: using Mrs Shakespeare and Nobody to show what might happen if a little touch of meditative awareness is added to the Bard's literary equation.

At this point, my Prologue stopped speaking, but it was not the end, merely a lengthy dramatic pause. He ceased to look at his scroll, gave the audience a friendly smile and engaged them more informally:

> *So... come with me, let me invite you*
> *With this small drama to excite you,*
> *And meet Will Shakespeare and his wife*
> *And give them both a different life.*
> *And what we poor players lack in skill*
> *Let your imagination now fulfill.*

One of the things I like about *A Midsummer Night's Dream* is the humble apology Puck offers at the end of the play, when he asks the audience to forgive the fact that a fantastic fairy tale has been offered on stage by ordinary actors:

```
If we shadows have offended
Think but this and all is mended,
That you did but slumber here
While these shadows did appear,
And this weak and idle theme
No more fleeting than a dream...
```

The same kind of thing happens in *Henry V* when the opening Chorus asks for 'a Muse of fire' to tell the story of the Battle of Agincourt, adding:

But pardon, gentles all,
The flat unraised spirits that have dared
On this unworthy scaffold to bring forth
So great an object...

It's a nice dramatic device that makes the audience feel good and that's why I included a similar apology at the beginning of my play. It reduces expectations, invites sympathy from the audience and asks them to become involved, supporting the story with their imagination.

One minor difference, though, between me and the Bard: he really didn't need to do it. I did.

Anand Subhuti

Chapter Three

Amleth to the Rescue

Will is in trouble. He has incurred Royal displeasure. This calamity occurs right at the beginning of my play. The aging Queen Elizabeth I stomps on to the stage, waving Shakespeare's recently-completed script of *Romeo and Juliet* in the air, barely able to contain herself.

"I will not have this play performed in my court, not while there is a single breath left in my body," she declares angrily. "No, no, no, Master Shakespeare!"

Will is freaked. He thought he'd hit the jackpot with this romantic tale. Instead, it looks like he's heading for the Tower. Pleadingly, in his best servile manner, the Bard tries to persuade his royal patron to change her mind.

"But Your Majesty, it is a worthy play..."

"I commanded a tragedy, Master Shakespeare."

"But *Romeo and Juliet* is a tragedy, Your Majesty."

Elizabeth gives a snort of Royal contemp. "Ha! Do you take me for a fool?"

Since no sane person, wishing to keeping his torso and head joined together, would ever dream of saying 'Yes' to such a question, Will's response is unsurprising:

"No indeed, Your Majesty."

"It is a love story, Master Shakespeare, and what is more, it is an *indecent* love story! Will you have me sit on my throne, in front of the entire court, and watch while a young girl, *barely 13 years old*, shares her *bed* with her *lover?*"

The queen savours her words, like feasting on forbidden fruit, the saliva of self-righteousness dripping from her mouth. It's not often that a frustrated old maid has the chance to use such pornographic language – well, porn to an Elizabethan prude, anyway.

It's a bit like the Clinton-Lewinsky scandal of the 90s, when Public Prosecutor Kenneth Starr's team of inquisitors relished extracting every salacious detail from poor Monica Lewinsky, urging her to confess exactly how Bill Clinton played with her breasts and in what manner she gave oral pleasure to the president's private parts. The prosecutors' insistence on laying bare the naked truth, lick by lick, mouthful by mouthful, was, of course, purely for the noble purpose of defending public morality.

"But they were married, Your Majesty," whimpers Will.

"A hasty, secret wedding, performed against all wise counsel. It cannot excuse the scandal you will have us watch."

Will has one last try. He pulls out his ace: the tragic ending.

"But they both die in the end, Your Majesty."

It doesn't work. He knew it. The Virgin Queen is having a full-on tantrum and nothing is going to mollify her.

"Too late, Master Shakespeare, much too late! The romance has already happened. I will have none of it!" To Will's horror, she rips up the manuscript and throws it on

     Anand Subhuti

the floor. As he instinctively bends to pick up the pieces, the Queen forbids it.

"Leave it there, I command you! And write me another play, to be performed within a week... or risk my deep displeasure. Do I make myself clear, Master Shakespeare?"

It's another no-brainer for the Bard. It's an historical fact that one of his relatives on his mother's side, a gentleman by the name of William Arden, was arrested for plotting against the Queen, sent to the Tower and executed. Therefore, mindful of the ease with which his own head might suddenly find itself separated from the rest of his mortal form, Master Shakespeare bows in slavish acquiescence.

"Very clear, Your Majesty."

The Queen storms out and Will, somewhat belatedly, has had enough of kissing royal ass. Thinking his patron is out of earshot, he declares loudly, "My God, what a bitch!"

But the Queen is blessed with acute hearing. She stops, turns slowly and inquires with deliberate menace:

"What did you say, Master Shakespeare?"

Will has slightly less than a nanosecond to avoid decapitation. His rhyming skills are urgently required to cast a smokescreen of confusion around the word 'bitch'. Smiling obsequiously, he stammers:

"Er... I said... that I am *rich*!

Your patronage prevents me...

From falling in a *ditch*!"

The Queen gives another contemptuous snort of displeasure and exits. Will is left alone on stage, but not for long. As he glumly begins to pick up the pieces of his torn script, two members of his theatre troupe come bounding in, full of good spirits, delighted to have the opportunity to tease the playwright – nothing like kicking a Bard when he's down.

These two players, by the way, are my real-life loving couple, who will shortly be slipping into the roles of Hamlet and Ophelia. But, right now, they are just a couple of actors in the Lord Chamberlain's Men – the name given to Shakespeare's drama troupe during the reign of Elizabeth.

One might speculate that such youthful players suffered under the Bard during long, tedious rehearsals of his works at The Globe, and therefore seized any opportunity to poke fun at him. They speak in rhyming couplets, which, for some reason, I find easy to compose. Hamlet is the First Player, Ophelia, the second:

First Player (gloating): "How now, what grave misfortune have we here?"

Second Player (ironically): "Her Majesty was not too pleased, I fear!"

First Player (with mock pity): "Why Will, what ails you man? Why this distress?"

Second Player (with feigned innocence): "Have you been fighting with our Royal Mistress?"

The luckless Bard is in no mood to jest:

"Leave me alone, good fellows, I entreat you.

I lack the time and humour now to meet you."

The two young players have no intention of leaving him alone. This is too good an opportunity to poke fun. Snatching up fragments of the torn script they take huge delight in over-acting the parts of *Romeo and Juliet*.

First Player (*playing Juliet*): "Oh Romeo, Romeo! Wherefore art thou Romeo?"

Second Player (*playing Romeo*): "But soft, what light

through yonder window breaks? It is the East and Juliet is the sun!"

First Player throws away her script and opens her arms wide in a passionate invitation: "Take me, Romeo, for I am yours!"

Second Player runs towards her crying, "My love! My angel!"

They collapse on the floor together in a passionate but comic embrace, engulfed by fits of laughter.

Will has had enough:

"Stop it, both of you! Leave me in peace.

For I must write a tragedy, within a week."

First Player (getting up): "What story will you tell? Hast thou begun?"

Shakespeare: "Alas, I know not. Inspiration have I none."

The two players look at each other and nod in unspoken agreement.

Second Player: "Will, we can help you..."

First Player: "...if you so desire."

Shakespeare is suspicious. "How now? What mischief do you two conspire?"

First Player: "Last month, in Denmark, we played before the king..."

Second Player: "In his great castle did we dance and sing..."

First Player: "A mighty feast was held, with many plays..."

Second Player: "Heroic tales and legends from the grave..."

First Player: "One story was admired above them all..."

Second Player: "The greatest tragedy, wherein a king did fall..."

First Player: "The king's own brother did most treacherously take his life..."

Second Player: "And then he forced the Queen to be his wife!"

Shakespeare's curiosity is roused. They have his attention. Might this obscure Danish folk tale offer, perhaps, the possibility of personal salvation?

"So far so good... and then?" he ventures.

First Player: "Then her poor son, Amleth, tortured by this stealth..."

Second Player: "Knows not whether to kill the new king, or himself..."

First Player: "And so he struggles on, quite desperately,"

Second Player: "Not knowing whether to be, or not to be."

Okay, I'm sure you get the picture. I set up the dramatic tension by putting Will under pressure from Queen Elizabeth, then introduce the concept of *Hamlet* as a solution. But I don't want Shakespeare to pull the idea out of thin air, because in real life things don't happen that way. All creators need inspiration and even the greatest minds need a trigger from which to fire off a new fantasy.

Historically, it may well have happened the way I'm describing it.

In the summer of 2012, I paid a visit to Kronborg Castle, near the Danish town of Helsingor. This was Shakespeare's *Elsinore Castle* where Hamlet was supposed to have lived. To tell the truth, I wasn't much interested in the place and would normally never have gone there. I'd come to Copenhagen to visit a beautiful Danish woman with whom I'd enjoyed a delightful love affair a few months earlier. I was eager to renew our sexual connection but to my dismay, upon my arrival, she announced that from now on she wanted us to be 'just good friends' – a phrase which, as we all know, conveys the kiss of death to any lover.

However, her desire to be with me was genuine. She really wanted us to be friends and begged me to stay, but I was in such a foul mood it didn't seem possible. In desperation, she suggested a trip to Kronborg as a distraction and I agreed, sulking all the way in the train. It was only when we got to the castle that I started to cheer up and take an interest in my surroundings.

Kronborg overlooks the Oresund Strait, a narrow strip of water that separates Denmark from Sweden. In the sixteenth century, from this vantage point, the kings of Denmark, backed by fleets of warships, imposed taxes on goods carried by every merchant vessel passing between the North Sea and the Baltic. The revenue was huge and placed them among the richest monarchs in Europe.

Even when the merchants tried to cheat by under-stating the value of their cargo, hoping to pay less duty, the kings foiled them by imposing the right to purchase goods carried in any ship at the price set by the merchants themselves.

The traders were royally screwed. If they declared the real value of their goods, they had to pay heavy taxes. If they tried to make the goods cheaper, the king would buy everything at the declared rate and make a handsome profit.

Anyway, all this wealth was lavished on Kronborg Castle. In Shakespeare's day, King Frederick II transformed his simple medieval fortress into a magnificent Renaissance castle and held great feasts there, accompanied by much dancing, singing and theatrical events. So did his successor, Christian IV.

While walking through the Great Hall where all this happened, I was told by our guide that Elizabethan players from London were occasionally hired by these Danish kings to perform at their feasts. Most probably, this is how a version of the famous Norse legend of *Amleth*, whose story-line closely follows that of Hamlet, reached London. Shakespeare picked up the idea from returning English thespians.

Good hypothesis? Well, if you ask me, it's a lot more plausible than some of the off-the-wall theories surrounding the Bard. Take, for example, the 2011 movie *Anonymous*, which claims to show how Edward de Vere, 17th Earl of Oxford, wrote Shakespeare's plays. I don't buy that for several reasons:

23. The noble earl inconveniently expired in 1604, before many of the plays were written.

24. Oxford happily published his own plays under his own name – humility and anonymity were not his strong suits.

25. He was the patron of his own troupe of players, the Earl of Oxford's Men, who were in direct competition with Shakespeare's company.

Moreover, as John Cleese and the creators of Monty Python would no doubt have observed, Edward de Vere showed every indication of being an 'upper class twit' with plenty of talent for sexual debauchery, losing money and sudden outbursts of violence, but little in the way of genius.

Advocates of the Oxford candidacy argue that Shakespeare wasn't cultured enough to be familiar with

    Anand Subhuti

the legends, history, folk tales and international gossip that make up the stories of his plays. What nonsense! Even an ordinary journalist like me, who once worked as a political reporter in the Houses of Parliament, could easily weave stories together out of rumour and gossip – in fact, that's what I was paid for. And I rather fancy, had I lived 400 years earlier, I could have done the same at Elizabeth's court, picking up tales from travellers coming from abroad and fashioning them into my own creations.

If a Fleet Street hack can do it, what to say of a poet like Shakespeare? Two London players return from a gig at Kronborg Castle, pass on the basics of a good tale to Will, and without difficulty Amleth becomes Hamlet. After all, it's the poetry and depth of human character that counts with Shakespeare, not the historical detail, with which the Bard improvised freely. How else would a bunch of English fairies – Oberon, Titania and Puck – find themselves in a Greek wood outside Athens in *A Midsummer Night's Dream?* It's bizarre, nothing to do with Greek culture, but it works wonderfully.

By the way, it's quite remarkable how certain myths find their way around the world. The legend of Amleth doesn't originate in Denmark. Earlier versions have been found in Byzantine, Greek and Roman myths, so you see how ideas move and mutate.

A couple more historical titbits:

1. Christian IV of Denmark was a cousin of King James I of England – who succeeded when Elizabeth died in 1603 – and the two enjoyed watching theatre together, including Shakespeare's plays. However, by the time the Danish king visited London in 1606, *Hamlet* had

already been written, so Christian wasn't the one who passed on the plot.

2. It's claimed that a play with Hamlet's theme existed in London prior to the Bard's epic, but, if so, it could have been similarly inspired – by players returning from the Danish court.

Basically, it's a great story. In the Danish version, Amleth is the son of Horwendil, King of Jutland. Horwendil is murdered by Feng, his brother – I love these Viking names – and then Feng becomes the new king and marries Horwendil's wife, Gerutha. Meanwhile, Amleth feigns madness to avoid being killed by Feng, then leaves the country, teams up with the King of England by marrying his daughter and invades Denmark. He burns the Great Hall, incinerating a large number of drunken nobles in the process, then slaughters his uncle, thereby avenging his father.

Stirring stuff! Clearly, Amleth was more a man of action than Hamlet, who, poor boy, was prone to long periods of intellectual agonising and little in the way of swashbuckling heroics.

And here, if you will, a small theatrical aside: I have to apologise for the way my two players explain the legend to Will, because, as you may have noticed, they say that Amleth was in mental torment, wondering whether to be or not to be. Not a chance. Amleth was a Viking, born and bred, and these gung-ho warriors were renowned for head-chopping, not mind-fucking. But I need to bring in the famous 'to be' line somewhere, so it will have to do. If Shakespeare can take liberties then, by god, so can I.

Listening to the tale told by these two players,

          Anand Subhuti

Shakespeare's mood changes from despair to hope. Out of the blue, they have thrown him a lifeline. Now he wants to hear the whole story, which he intends to shamelessly plagiarise in order to meet the Queen's deadline.

"It is a worthy tale, what happens next?" he asks.

But it's not going to be that easy. The two players scratch their heads, look at each other and affect mischievous ignorance.

"Er... we forget," says one.

"Oh no!" Shakespeare throws his hands up in frustration, until they reassure him thus:

First Player: "It matters not, Will, draw upon thy skill..."

Second Player: "And let your clever mind write what you will."

First Player: "Just make it up, you shall invent the rest."

Second Player (*smirking with irony*): "After all, it is what you do best!"

First Player: "As long as they all die when the play ends..."

Second Player: "The Queen will love you..."

First Player (*rubbing her fingers to indicate money*): "...and make sweet amends!"

The Bard is convinced. After all, he really doesn't have much choice if he is to write, produce and perform a finished drama in seven days. The die is cast.

Shakespeare: "It shall be done. I'll write this 'Hamlet' now.

For I must save my precious neck somehow!

Henceforth, Will Shakespeare's plays shall ever be, Remembered for their gloom and tragedy!"

Chapter Four

Heros, Zeros, Kings and Villains

I think of my play as... well... a play. But, to be more accurate, it's a musical. Or maybe it's a bit of both. Strictly speaking, it doesn't conform to the musical genre, because although it has enough songs to qualify, there's too much dialogue.

The first musical I saw was the counter-culture rock musical *Hair* which I caught up with in London in the late 60s. As you can imagine, its anti-establishment offering of sexual freedom and illegal drugs was immensely appealing to me as a young man, fresh out of university and now working as a straight journalist during the week, while mutating into a dope-smoking hippie at the weekends.

Hair, like most musicals, had minimal dialogue and plot development. It had sensationalism, for sure – guaranteed by the nude scene – but its main strength was its songs, many of which were embraced by the anti-Vietnam-war movement in the States.

The most recent musical I saw was *Mamma Mia*, which I must confess I enjoyed in spite of its mildly nauseating 'feel good' nature. Somehow, for me, any song written by

Björn Ulvaeus and Benny Andersson has that 'nice and wholesome' feeling, all clean and tidy, like a Swedish village on a Sunday morning. Even when Bjorn and Benny are trying to be deep, they end up on the surface.

I didn't see the stage show, but felt pulled to the movie by an irresistible force: for the life of me, I couldn't visualize a talented actress like Meryl Streep agreeing to take part in a sugar-coated reprise of Abba's hits. I had to check it out.

Sure enough, there was Streep, living in a villa on the mythical Greek island of Kalokairi, convincing me that, yes, any of three men could be the father of her daughter and, yes, this confusion offered a perfectly good reason for her to sing *The Winner Takes It All*.

What I'm saying is that, generally speaking, musicals are short on dialogue and sketchy in plot, using just enough of both to string the songs together. My offering, on the other hand, contained lots of dialogue and a detailed story line, so the addition of seven songs made it a strange beast, neither one thing nor the other.

The opening number occurs immediately after the Bard's decision to write the tragedy of Hamlet. The whole cast comes onstage and forms a chorus line, except for the Queen, who stands apart and listens while the rest of us sing:

> *Another drama for you to see,*
> *Another ending in misery,*
> *It's oh-so tragic, it has to be*
> *It's for her Royal Majesty.*
>
> *Another drama to make you sad,*
> *Another story that's going bad*
> *If you enjoy it*

You must be mad!
It's for her Royal Majesty.

Heroes, zeroes, kings and villains
Kill each other with precision.
Cleopatra's destiny
Dying with Mark Anthony,
Juliet as we all know
Killed herself for Romeo,
Star-crossed lovers, heartbreak endings
Tragedy and gloom descending
Is there more that we can't see?
Is this all that's meant to be?

Another drama for you to see,
Another ending in misery,
It's oh-so tragic, it has to be
It's for her Royal Majesty.
Another drama to make you sad,
Another story that's going bad
If you enjoy it
You must be mad!
It's for her Royal Majesty... we're going crazeeeeeeee!
It's for her Royal Majesty.

The tone is ironic. Really, it's a kind of complaint, sung by a troupe of players who are being forced to be gloomy against their will; hence the hook line: 'It's for her Royal Majesty...' Each time we sang it, the whole chorus line bowed humbly in her direction, emphasizing our lack of choice.

But I don't allow gloom without humour, so we created a pantomime to illustrate the absurdity of it all:

 Anand Subhuti

Heroes, zeroes, kings and villains, kill each other with precision...

The two attendants walked forward and, with clockwork military precision, turned to face each other, drew their swords and ran each other through the guts, sinking down together in a crumpled heap.

Cleopatra's destiny, dying with Mark Anthony...

Mrs Shakespeare and I walked forward and she performed a classic faint, a dying swan, passing away elegantly in my arms, while I clasped my forehead in mock despair.

Juliet as we all know, killed herself for Romeo...

Hamlet and Ophelia walked forward and she died in his arms, stabbing herself with an imaginary dagger. With piles of neatly paired corpses, we made our point:

Star-crossed lovers, heartbreak endings...

And here, we added what to me was a delightful touch, using only male voices, going deeper and deeper, slower and slower, with:

Tragedy and gloom descending...

So with 'descending' we ended up in the deepest basement of gloom and doom.

By the way, we didn't actually sing. A week earlier, we'd all hopped in a taxi and were driven to a Christian theological college in another suburb of Pune to meet Father Edwin, the quietly efficient manager-producer of the college's recording studio.

I don't know why the college had a studio. Maybe it was for nuns to sing devotional chorales in their high, pure, soprano voices, or monks growling *Te Deums* in basso profundo tones. Anyway, a couple of musicians at the Resort turned me onto it as the only reasonably-priced studio within striking range of the ashram. They assured me that Father Edwin was not averse to helping Osho sannyasins, even though our approach to spirituality might not be – how shall I say? – in perfect synchronicity with his own theological views.

His studio looked retro, like something out of the 60s, but was impressive, with soundproof rooms, an endless supply of microphones and bundles of cords, and a mixing board offering god-knows how many tracks, illuminated by rows of pinhead-sized green and red lights. The whole thing had an 'Abbey Road' feel to it, as if George Martin might walk in any moment and start working on a track from *Sergeant Pepper's Lonely Hearts Club Band.*

And so, while Jesus gazed down upon us from his cross on the wall, we recorded *It's For Her Royal Majesty* and other would-be show-stoppers. This meant, of course, that we would be lip-synching the songs during our live action onstage, which was fine by me.

Only one of us was good enough to sing live and that was my Swedish actress wife, who, in one of her many showbiz incarnations, had once been part of a fairly successful, all-female, electro-punk band. Queen Elizabeth had a decent enough voice, too, but the rest of us were useless.

As for me, I could hold a tune only with constant practice, which I gained by picking up the mike at the Resort's weekly karaoke event and – ignoring groans from my long-suffering friends – singing songs requiring little vocal range, like the Eurythmics *Sweet Dreams Are Made of This* or Simon and Garfunkel's *The Sound of Silence.* It was only after months of cautious progress that I dared to sing my all-time favourite karaoke number, the fast,

     Anand Subhuti

rock 'n roll, tongue-twister *Johnny B. Goode*, penned by the immortal Chuck Berry.

On that fateful night, after I'd put down the microphone, a well-wishing musician friend came up to me and whispered, "You sang the whole song out of key. I thought you'd want to know that."

Thanks.

So, with only one professional in the cast, we had no option but to pre-record all the numbers. And, besides, we couldn't trust our rented radio mics to produce anything like the sound quality required.

Two decades earlier, pop-rock pioneer Madonna had paved the way for using live, chic, headset mics – not to mention pink, cone-shaped brassieres – with her iconic *Blond Ambition* tour, but we, alas, lacked the vocal talent to dare to follow in her footsteps.

Over to you, Father Edwin...

Chapter Five

The World is an Illusion

Hamlet walks on stage carrying a skull. He spies Will Shakespeare, sitting in an old-fashioned chair, hunched over his manuscript, his quill pen racing over the parchment on his lap as he strives to compose his masterpiece.

As the Bard, I'm on stage the whole time, throughout the play. I wrote it that way, which could make me a megalomaniac writer-director-actor, but, as a theatrical device it works pretty well. Shakespeare's presence lends continuity to the storyline, which, as I mentioned earlier, draws its pace and dramatic tension from his urgent need to please Queen Elizabeth before she cuts off his head. Anyway, that's my excuse.

Hamlet strolls across the stage, coming close to Will, inadvertently thrusting the skull in the Bard's face. In the original play, of course, this skull is the last remains of Yorick, whose transformation from 'a fellow of infinite jest' into a decaying set of dentures provides Hamlet with yet another opportunity for lengthy melancholic musings on the futility of life, commencing with the famous line:

"Alas poor Yorick! I knew him, Horatio..."

 Anand Subhuti

Somehow, this grave aside – if you'll excuse the pun – has remained fixed in people's minds, generation after generation. Even today, when you google the word 'alas', Yorick pops up as one of your first options.

In my play, however, the arrival of a skull onstage has yet to be explained. Hamlet waits to be noticed by the busy playwright and then, when he is not, coughs impatiently to make his presence known.

"Ahem...excuse me, Will."

Will looks up from his writing and is confronted by two hollow eye sockets staring blankly at him. He freaks.

"Aaaargh! For god's sake, man, what do you think you're doing?"

"Sorry, Will. I've come for the audition."

"What?"

"The part. I've come to play Hamlet."

"But why the skull?"

"Well, you said it's a tragedy, so I brought along my grandfather to add a little atmosphere."

Will recovers his composure, takes the skull from Hamlet and inspects it curiously. "Oh, very well. After all, if I fail to please the Queen, this is what I will look like in a week!"

He puts down the skull by the side of his chair, fumbles through his manuscript, pondering over what he's written, then hands a piece of parchment to Hamlet. Getting up, Will takes Hamlet by the hand and brings him to centre stage.

"Stand here, face the audience and read this."

Hamlet holds the script before him, striking a dramatic, overly-theatrical pose that reminds me of Laurence Olivier, who, in 1948 brought *Hamlet* to the silver screen and in so doing won the only Academy Award ever given to an actor playing a Shakespearian role.

However, I'm forced to disagree with the Oscar-givers, because Olivier never impressed me as an actor, even when, as a teenager, I saw him play Othello at the Chichester Festival Theatre in Sussex, in 1964. For me, he was an orator, not an actor. He had a wonderful voice and could stride around a stage, delivering epic lines in ringing tones, but with little genuine emotion. Even when murdering his beautiful wife, Desdemona, brushing off his jealousy with 'It is the cause, it is the cause, my soul', I couldn't feel his passion in it.

A black man killing a white woman? That scene should have set the world on fire. But, no, we had to wait another 30 years before O.J. Simpson fulfilled this scenario's headline-gripping potential.

Sir Larry was old school, pre-Method. He could *act* his characters, but he couldn't *be* them. That's what made it so humiliating for him to play alongside Marilyn Monroe in *The Prince and the Showgirl* in 1957. Up close to the camera, he lacked the ability to convey his feelings, whereas Monroe oozed emotional authenticity in every scene.

It's one of those oddities of destiny that Olivier's name has become synonymous with good acting. The annual awards for excellence in London plays and shows are now called the Olivier Awards.

The bust on the award does, however, depict Olivier as Henry V, a straightforward action role in which he was much more comfortable. And, let's face it, a play about the English beating the crap out of the French can't fail in the United Kingdom, neither in Shakespeare's time nor our own. The fact that the Battle of Agincourt was an isolated

     Anand Subhuti

victory in a ruinous, century-long war in which England lost almost all its French possessions is conveniently ignored by the Bard and everyone else.

Another peeve about Olivier: it's hard to forgive his introductory comment, at the start of his *Hamlet* movie, where he announces: "This is the tragedy of a man who cannot make up his mind."

Whoa! That's way too banal for my taste, Sir Larry. It's like saying *Macbeth* is the story of a henpecked husband, or *Romeo and Juliet* is about a young couple with family problems. Which makes me wonder: did Olivier have any depth at all, or was he just a voice?

Meanwhile, onstage in Pune, Hamlet begins his audition, clearing his throat and loudly proclaiming the most famous line in the history of theatre:

"To be, or not to be, that is..."

He pauses, shrugs and laughs... "*such* a stupid question!"

Will is gobsmacked. He can't believe his ears.

"What do you mean, man?" he asks angrily. Shakespeare has just posed the deepest philosophical question that his brilliant mind can imagine, and this young creep blows it off like a cheap slogan for a TV commercial.

"Explain yourself!" he demands.

"Nobody asks questions like this, Will."

Offended and indignant, Will shakes his head. "I don't believe this! You and your colleague gave me that line yourselves, from the play in Denmark!"

Hamlet shrugs, conveying his indifference to the alleged brilliance of the line. "I guess it sounds better in Danish."

Highly miffed, Will stabs an authoritarian finger at

the parchment in Hamlet's hand. "Just read the script," he orders, testily. His ego as London's literary-genius-in-residence has been deeply dented.

Dutifully, Hamlet completes the audition, declaring:

> "Whether 'tis nobler in the mind to suffer
> The slings and arrows of outrageous fortune,
> Or to take arms against a sea of troubles,
> And by opposing end them."

He gets the part. Of course he does. In real life, as I already mentioned, he and Ophelia are deeply in love, so they come as a package. Moreover, we are obliged to do all our rehearsing in the living room of their apartment as we don't have any other space in this over-crowded city. So, one way or another, he's hired.

Now, let's fast forward from Elizabethan England, or rewind from the present-day, and pay a visit – if you will – to a stuffy classroom at a high school in the south of England, where a 17-year-old boy is reading the part of Hamlet.

I remember the date exactly: it is October 24, 1962, and happens to be my birthday. The Cuban Missile Crisis is at its peak and somewhere, far away in Washington and Moscow, John F. Kennedy and Nikita Kruschev are contemplating blowing the world to pieces.

It happened more than half a century ago and nobody bothers about it now. But allow me to remind you: never, in the long chronicle of madness we call history, have we ever come so close to destroying the human race as we did in 1962. The two world wars that preceded it were just parlour games compared to the shit that was about to come down on *homo sapiens*. Hundreds of megaton nukes were poised, aimed and ready to fly in a push-button apocalypse.

"To be or not to be..."

I remember reciting that line aloud while secretly thinking, "Who the fuck cares?"

To be accurate, I probably didn't use the f-word. The social usefulness and linguistic flexibility of 'fuck' had yet to be introduced to me. But, still, I remember that moment. I couldn't articulate what I was feeling, but it was as if a curtain was being lifted, revealing my own rebellious intelligence, which until then had been hidden – even from me – behind an unquestioning acceptance of whatever was being taught to me under the guise of education.

I saw the difference between the intellectual and the existential. Hamlet's oh-so-profound question was a mind-fuck. It appeared to be deep but it wasn't. In fact, in that moment, the whole laborious process of British education seemed utterly phony to me.

What was real, what was pulsating as an invisible presence in our little classroom, filled with nicely-uniformed schoolboys and a fusty old teacher with chalk dust on his gown, was the very real possibility that suddenly, without warning, we would all be vaporised by a nuclear blast. My birthday might be my deathday.

Maybe for Nikita Khrushchev the question was real. *To be or not to be?* If that pig-faced little Russian had opted for *not to be* we'd have all been toast, or perished slowly in the ensuing nuclear winter. One minor consequence of the fall-out from such an epic event, by the way, would be that you wouldn't be sitting where you are now, reading this book.

So, that's when I started to figure out the difference between thinking and living.

To be or not to be? Eventually, I came to the conclusion that *not to be* is the only way to be. But this paradoxical insight comes later in my tale.

Chapter Six

Free To Be Me

Mrs Shakespeare is looking at me with a bright, sardonic smile, as if seeking answers while knowing that whatever I tell her is going to be ridiculous. Perhaps she is right. Mrs Shakespeare is free from the influence of politics and not afraid to speak her mind – especially to her husband.

The location for this scene is the Bard's household and Mrs Shakespeare, going about her wifely duties, has stumbled across the ongoing Hamlet audition. Here, I insert a freeze-frame in the audition itself, so that the Bard's wife can have her say.

"So, let me get this straight," she muses, inspecting the solitary young man standing motionless in the middle of the stage. "This handsome-looking young man is called Hamlet..."

"Right," says Will.

"Hamlet's father was the King of Denmark, but the king was killed by his brother. The brother becomes the new King of Denmark and marries Hamlet's... mother?"

"Right," says Will. When his wife is speaking, Will keeps his answers short. I wrote the script that way – you can't

     Anand Subhuti

say I didn't learn anything from my love relationships with the opposite sex.

"Hamlet wants to kill the new king, to revenge his father, but instead spends a long time wondering whether to be or not to be, which makes everything very complicated. And how does it all end...?"

"In tragedy," says Will.

As if she doesn't know. Mrs Shakespeare is a wise woman. She knows all about her husband's dilemma. She knows that Queen Elizabeth is a bitter, angry old woman who is forcing her husband and his troupe of players to perform dramas that end only in suffering and death.

Historically, it's not true. The Virgin Queen seems to have enjoyed comedy as much as tragedy. But I'm using her to make a point: Shakespeare became England's greatest playwright, revered down the centuries, because people were impressed with his tragedies.

Humour doesn't count. Even today you can see it, in Hollywood's annual glam-fest known as the Oscars. It's the actors playing 'serious' roles who usually bag the gongs. Dustin Hoffman won his pair for *Rain Man* and *Kramer vs. Kramer*, not for his brilliant, gender-bending, comic performance as *Tootsie*. Renee Zellweger won hers for *Cold Mountain*, a tear-jerking war drama, not for her hilarious portrayal of Bridget Jones. Sometimes the things we respect most do us the most harm.

Meanwhile, back on stage, my wife is about to drive home this point, with needle-like precision:

"Hamlet dies...?" she asks.

"Yes," says Will.

"Hamlet's mother dies?"

"Yes."

"The new king dies?"

"Yes."

"The king's prime minister dies?"

"Yes."

"The king's prime minister's son dies?"

"Yes."

Our one-sided dialogue is interrupted by a vision of loveliness, a hauntingly beautiful figure who glides slowly across the stage. I was right: Savita is stunningly charismatic as the heartbroken, doomed Ophelia.

Mrs Shakespeare pauses and takes her in, appreciating, along with the audience, this gorgeous sacrificial pawn, ghost-like with her pale face and scarlet lips, soft and vulnerable in her white, flowing gown.

"And who might this young lady be?"

"This is Ophelia, the Prime Minister's daughter. She's madly in love with Hamlet."

"Ah, something to be happy about, at last!"

Will is forced to disillusion his wife, who, one suspects, already knows that happiness is not a major theme in this politically-driven saga. "Not exactly," says the Bard, cautiously. "You see, the murder of his father has driven Hamlet almost mad, so he rejects Ophelia. Watch and see!"

Hamlet, who has been standing motionless all this time, suddenly comes to life and, true to form, cruelly abuses his former beloved. Here, for a few lines, we stick to the Bard's original script:

Hamlet *(sneering disdainfully at his former love)* "I did love thee once."

Ophelia *(nursing her wounded heart)* "Indeed, my lord, you made me believe so."

Hamlet *(callously)*: "You should not have believe me, I loved thee not!

    Anand Subhuti

Ophelia (*stricken with grief*): "Alas, I was the more deceived!"

And this, as we all know, is where Hamlet loses it, screaming:

"Get thee to a nunnery! Why wouldst thou be a breeder of sinners? Or, if thou wouldst marry, marry a fool, for wise men know well enough what monsters you make of them. To a nunnery go, and quickly, too! Farewell!"

Ophelia sobs and sinks to the floor in despair. Mrs Shakespeare waits for Hamlet's tirade to end and then returns to her task of husband-hunting.

By the way, maybe I should tell you, Mrs Shakespeare is not your stereotypical Swedish blonde. As I mentioned earlier, she has dark brown hair, penetrating blue eyes and the kind of neutral face which, while attractive in its own right, can be made up as a clown, a femme fatale, an innocent child, or an Elizabethan housewife.

She's got that chameleon quality of an experienced actress and for this reason her presence always makes me feel slightly unsettled. I'm never sure who I'm with. I can't grab hold of her personality and fix it. In a way, our relationship nicely mirrors that of Mr and Mrs Shakespeare – Will can never be sure whose side his wife is on.

By now, you will have realized that my portrayal of 'Mrs S' has little to do with the Bard's historical wife, Anne Hathaway, about whom we know virtually nothing, apart from the fact that she was eight years older than her husband, bore him three children and was famously bequeathed the family's 'second-best bed' in her husband's will.

No, our Mrs Shakespeare is an entirely different creature, far more dangerous than the obscure Ms Hathaway, and right now she's on a roll, so we'd better get back to the action.

"So Hamlet told Ophelia he loved her, and now he doesn't... and now what will she do?" she asks her husband.

Will would love to escape at this point, but all the exits are blocked. He is cornered. He has no choice but to be struck by the twin arrows of irony and sarcasm now speeding towards his chest, shot from his wife's verbal bow.

"Er... she will throw herself in a lake."

"And drown herself and die?"

"Yes, in her grief and her despair."

Long dramatic pause. "Will...," she says slowly.

"Hmmm...?"

"Don't you think you're overdoing it, just a teeny bit? All this doom and gloom...?"

Just a teeny bit. Mrs Shakespeare's use of understatement is superb, especially when one considers that this was the longest of all the Bard's plays, a four-hour marathon of nonstop misery. In fact, she hates the whole idea of *Hamlet* and is determined to rescue all the characters and transform them into happy human beings. Her campaign begins with Ophelia.

But first, Will has to fight a short, hopeless rearguard action.

"The Queen will love it," he protests.

"Yes, well, the Queen is 67 years old and still a virgin," retorts his wife. "But what about all the young women who will watch your play? *Get thee to a nunnery...? Breeder of sinners...?* What kind of example are you giving them?"

Will waves a dismissive hand while uttering the classic cliché used by all men who are forced to surrender to feminine wisdom while pretending to remain intellectually superior.

 Anand Subhuti

"Oh, you don't understand, woman!"

Mrs Shakespeare is not impressed. "Oh, but I rather think I do. Come here, sweetheart," she murmurs, taking the poor girl by the hand and raising her up. "Now listen, you're much too young to go drowning yourself in a lake."

Ophelia turns her beautiful head to cast a soulful look in the direction of Hamlet.

"But... but I love him!"

"Yes, well, there are plenty more idiots where that one came from I assure you," retorts Mrs Shakespeare in a brisk, no-nonsense manner. "Now what you need is a role model..."

Ophelia is puzzled. "What's a role model?" she asks.

By way of reply, Mrs Shakespeare turns and speaks directly to the audience, in one of several theatrical asides she will deliver during this performance.

"Oh, I forgot, that phrase doesn't come into fashion for another 400 years..." she again faces Ophelia. "Well, someone to look up to... someone to give you hope... someone to show you a new vision of life."

Ophelia is bewildered. "Like who?" she wonders.

Mrs Shakespeare thinks for a moment. Then it dawns on her. "How about Lady Raga?"

I have to confess, when I wrote the first draft of this play, I had Mrs Shakespeare say "How about Lady Gaga?" Gaga was an obvious choice, a symbol of young, rebellious, *do-anything-I-fucking-well-please-onstage* female liberation. Of course, this was a few years back, before Miley Cyrus eclipsed Gaga by swinging naked on a wrecking ball, then twerking onstage with American singer Robin Thicke. Now Gaga's envelope-pushing dramatics seem positively conservative.

Anyway, I was going to have Ophelia sing Gaga's hit number *Bad Romance* to Hamlet, then turn away from him and proclaim her independence by singing *Born This Way*.

However, it's better to be original whenever possible, especially when it comes to avoiding royalty fees, so I composed two new songs for the occasion and also changed the name of the role model from Gaga to 'Raga' for my India-savvy audience. As many of you know, a *raga* is a piece of classical Indian music, so it was a perfect *double entendre*.

Two courtly attendants, dressed Elizabethan style, bring on a purple curtain which they hold up in front of Ophelia while, with Mrs Shakespeare's help, the young woman does a quick onstage change.

Funky, bluesy music begins to play and then Ophelia rips away the curtain and struts out towards the audience, dressed in a glitzy white tank top and matching mini-shorts, with white stockings. It's an all-blonde outfit and looks sensational. This is where the plot comes unglued and Will starts having a coronary arrest.

"Hey, what's going on? This isn't in my script!" he exclaims, but no one is listening, least of all Ophelia, who belts out the blues:

> *Raga and her Baba, we don't get along,*
> *Raga and her Baba, this man he done me wrong.*
> *Broke my heart in pieces and threw it on the floor,*
> *Still I come back crying, begging him for more...*
> *It's a crying shame... oooh yes it is... it's a crying shame...*

I wrote the lyrics and a Russian musician in St. Petersburg, a friend of mine called Ravi, did a great job adding the tune. One of the advantages of my lifestyle is

     Anand Subhuti

that I'm connected with a worldwide network of talented and artistic people – Ravi is one of them. He's in his mid-forties and does his best to look sad and mournful, like a soulful musician should, burdened by his own penetrating insights into the injustices to be found Russian society – we won't even mention the name 'Putin' in this context.

But by nature, Ravi is a bliss-addicted, happy-go-lucky sannyasin. Rather like Leonard Cohen, the melancholic Canadian songwriter and musician, he found that, in spite of discovering many excellent reasons to be depressed about the state of humanity, "cheerfulness kept breaking through". That's Ravi.

As I indicated earlier, Ophelia is lip-synching. It's actually Mrs Shakespeare's fine voice with which she moans onstage about her obsession with her *Baba*.

Ophelia has a highly individual way of dancing. It's odd. It's... well... a kind of sensual wriggle, arms and legs going everywhere at once, and no amount of choreography will change it. But somehow it works. She's all over Hamlet, slinking up to him, grabbing him then pushing him away, blaming him for her unrequited love. He's the *Baba* she's singing about:

> *Raga and her Baba, the man I love to hate,*
> *Raga and her Baba, a passion that can't wait.*
> *Broke my heart in pieces and threw it on the fire,*
> *Still I come back crying, burning with desire...*
> *It's a crying shame... oooh yes it is... it's a crying shame...*

Mrs Shakespeare, coaching from the sidelines, watches her protégé drape herself on Hamlet and slide erotically down his body in a masochistic gesture of addiction, then the older woman intervenes, stopping the music.

"You've got the right idea, sweetheart," she encourages Ophelia, "but you're still focusing on Hamlet. Take all the energy back and give it to yourself." She pauses for a moment, takes Ophelia's hands, looks lovingly into her eyes and delivers the key line: "You are free to be you."

Ophelia gasps in astonishment and delight at this unexpected gift, liberating her from the Bard's cruel pen. "Free to be me?" she echoes.

Cue for a song, if ever there was one. Mrs Shakespeare drags Hamlet to the side of the stage and Ophelia stands alone, facing the audience. After a moment of silence, a solo Spanish guitar comes in, flamenco-style, strumming dramatically in the background as Ophelia slowly and powerfully sings:

> *It's not the first time that you've made me cry,*
> *It's not the first time that you've said goodbye,*
> *But this time I have found a golden key,*
> *Without you, I have freedom... to be me...*

There's a sudden surge of music with a driving beat and Ophelia breaks into a fast rock tune, titled *Free To Be Me*, again composed by the Subhuti-Ravi team:

> *I'm free to be me, yeah, free to be me,*
> *Free to be me, yeah, free to be me...*
> *Free to say "No!" and free to say "Yes!"*
> *Free say "Hi!" and "Goodbye!" to the rest*
> *Free to cut loose and dance all night long*
> *Grab any guy and this is my song.*

While Hamlet watches in astonishment, Ophelia takes advantage of her new-found freedom to flirt with the two attendants who, along with Mrs Shakespeare, are doing

     Anand Subhuti

a pretty-damn-cool backing routine, wearing shades and strutting their stuff in time to the music. One of them, of course, is my oh-so-English Prologue, whose transformation into an MTV disco dancer adds comedy to the chorus line.

Ophelia homes in on the guys and flirts shamelessly with them:

> *Free to say "Hi, I'm single and free,"*
> *Free to say "You! You're coming with me!"*
> *Free to say "Guy, are you looking at me?"*
> *Free to say "Yeah, now, you're coming with me!"*
> *I'm free to be me, yeah, free to be me,*
> *Free to be me, yeah, free to be me...*

As the song fades, the two attendants lift her up and carry her off, while she waves glamorously to the audience, obviously ecstatic about her new-found freedom.

Okay, I admit, theatrically speaking, it's a bit of a stretch, switching so fast from helpless victim to liberated superwoman. But personal transformation is like that. One moment you're trapped inside a belief about yourself that grips your heart and mind so totally you can't imagine escaping from its clutches. Next moment, you're free to fly like an eagle across the sun, leaving no footprints in the blue sky – two metaphors frequently used by Osho to describe the state of spiritual liberation.

So, early in my play, Ophelia has a euphoric moment of liberation. But it's not going to be that easy. This young woman has greater challenges to face if she is to succeed in avoiding her dreadful fate. Queen Elizabeth, the all-powerful, all-miserable, all-English sovereign, has commanded a tragedy and, by god, that's what Will is determined to give her – if only to save his own neck. The Bard, you will note, is a pragmatist, not an idealist.

But he's up against his own wife, a highly resourceful and clever woman, so he's squeezed between a rock and a hard place.

This is how I set up the dramatic tension to carry the play towards it climax: Who is going to win? Mrs Shakespeare or the Queen? How does Will get out of this dilemma? Can Hamlet and Ophelia find true love? And what, you may be wondering, does all this have to do with meditation and starting a revolution of the soul?

Well, as the working men of Athens said to Duke Theseus in *A Midsummer Night's Dream*, when presenting their 'merry and tragical' play about Pyramus and Thisbe: "Wonder on, till truth make all things plain..."

 Anand Subhuti

Chapter Seven

Meanwhile, Behind the Curtain

Okay, now that we are well into the plot, I can tell you how this play came to be written. It began with a vision, or a fantasy... or maybe it was just a scam. Sometimes it's hard to tell the difference. Sometimes all three can be true together.

Anyway, one year previously, out of the blue, I'd received an invitation to participate in an Osho Arts Festival in Delhi, including several nights of cultural entertainment, presented by disciples of Osho, featuring a musical concert, a classical Indian dance performance and a theatre play. The general idea was to show the world how talented, creative and artistic Osho's sannyasins can be.

The festival was to take place in a modern auditorium with a seating capacity for 5,000 people. We would be flown to Delhi from Pune and we would stay in three-or-four-star hotels. All expenses would be paid. And I was being invited to provide a play for the evening of drama. It sounded great.

At first, I had no doubts about the festival, although the presence of a slight knot of tension in my stomach informed me that I had considerable doubts about my ability to produce a play to match the occasion. Searching for a quick solution, I thought back to the musical shows I'd written and staged in the 90s, wondering if perhaps one of them might do the job:

The Professor Who Lost His Mind. The tale of an American psychology professor who, accompanied by his wife and two children, goes inside his own mind to rescue his beautiful 'inner woman' from his male chauvinistic 'inner man'.

The Beautiful Princess. The story of a medieval prince and princess whose families hate each other and who find true love by making a Tardis-style time trip to the Pune ashram and doing past-life regression therapy.

Amrapali & the Wheel of Dharma. A beautiful courtesan from the days of Gautam Buddha emerges from a 2,500 year-old sleep to do battle with a power-mad Tibetan lama over who should control the next turn of the Wheel of Dharma.

Meet Me in Maroon. Four meditators at the Pune ashram try to save the world from a space vampire who threatens to suck the life out of the human race if they won't give him the secret of 'the key of life'.

All four musicals were comedies and all had been well received, when performed at the ashram. But there was a problem. It was indigenous theatre, written by a sannyasin, performed by sannyasins, for sannyasin audiences. Not necessarily the kind of thing that would be appreciated by a sophisticated audience in the Indian capital.

I'd also written a play called *Journey to Mount Kailash*, based on a true incident in Kathmandu, Nepal, in which a friend of mine, wrongfully jailed for smuggling heroin, tried to prove his innocence by trapping the woman who

     Anand Subhuti

set him up, with grudging cooperation from his jailer – a sceptical police inspector. But, again, not really the kind of thing to stage in an Osho Arts Festival.

To be relevant, our theatre show had to convey some aspect of Osho's mystical vision while keeping people entertained and also – most crucially – avoiding the awful trap of proselytizing. Nobody needed, or wanted, to have Osho rammed down their throats, and I certainly didn't want to be guilty of it.

It was my own memory of Osho's daily discourses that gave me the key. Over the years, I'd listened to a lot of them and I recalled several occasions on which the mystic had toyed with Shakespeare's most famous quote: *To be or not to be.*

For example, in 1987, responding to a question from a friend of mine about the significance of the Bard's utterance, Osho said:

Shakespeare is a great poet, but not a mystic. He has an intuition into the reality of things, but that is only a glimpse, very vague as if seen in a dream, not clear. His question in Hamlet shows that unclarity. 'To be or not to be?' can never be asked by a man who knows, because there is no question of choice. You cannot choose between 'to be' or 'not to be'.

In existential terms, not to be is the only way to be. Unless you disappear you are not really there. It looks a little difficult to understand, because basically it is irrational. But reason is not the way of existence; existence is as irrational as you can conceive.

Here, those who think they are, are not. And those who think and realize they are not – they are.

The idea that 'I am' is just an idea, a projection of the mind. But the realization that 'I am not' comes only as a flowering of meditation. When you realize, 'I am not', only the 'I' disappears and there remains behind a pure existence, undefined, unbounded, unfettered, just a pure space.

'I' is a great prison.

It is your slavery and bondage to the mind.

The moment you enter beyond the mind, you are – but you don't have any notion of being an ego, of being an 'I'. In other words: the more you think you are, the less you are; the more you experience that you are not... the more you are.

The moment the soap bubble of your ego pops, you have become the whole existence.

Osho's comments gave me the clue. I would use Hamlet's dilemma to contrast Western intellectual attitudes with Eastern spirituality. I would challenge the West's faith in the rational mind, opening the way for the East's insight into 'No Mind'.

In a way, I was challenging my own past. I had studied philosophy at university, steadily chewing my way through the works of Locke, Berkeley, Hume, Descartes, Rousseau, Kant, Hegel...Only to realize, after encountering Eastern mysticism, that the effort by all of these philosophers to find truth via the workings of the human mind was a waste of time. Not only was the mind the wrong tool for the job. Mind itself was the barrier.

Also, I was determined to write a comedy, off-setting Shakespeare's morbid play with a more positive, humorous and upbeat vision of life.

Most people think that if you're going to use art to present weighty issues, like East versus West, then you need to create something serious. But I disagree. I want people to laugh, chuckle and enjoy themselves, *and* take home something to think about.

So that's how I came up with my tale. On one level, it

Anand Subhuti

was about Will Shakespeare's dilemma of being forced by Queen Bess to kill off his characters, while his wife did her best to prevent him. On a deeper level, it showed how his characters could escape their fate by using meditation to change their beliefs. And at the deepest level it was a dismissal of the whole Western way of thinking.

But still, even if such a play could work as a piece of theatre, there were things about the Delhi Arts Festival that didn't seem plausible. For one thing, you cannot put on a play in front of an audience of 5,000 people. It won't work. Most of them will be seated too far away from the stage and, even with amplification, you will lose them.

Even Sir Larry, playing at Chichester, didn't have to face more than 1200 people. Rock superstars like Mick Jagger and Sting can handle audiences that size with massive towers of speakers, but not actors, and certainly not a bunch of amateurs with an obscure play. After a while, people are bound to feel restless, start chatting among themselves, coughing, scratching, checking their mobiles, walking out...

For us, it would be challenging enough to perform in a small, intimate theatre with a maximum of 500 people – 250 would be better.

Besides, I'd already burned my fingers in Delhi, back in the 70s, when I was part of a travelling group of players called The Rajneesh Shakespeare Company, offering two of the Bard's plays, *A Midsummer Night's Dream* and *As You Like It*.

Basically, it was a PR exercise – conceived by yours truly and okayed by Osho – aimed at offsetting the ashram's notorious reputation as a place of nonstop 'free love' where we ran around naked all day, having sex with multiple partners. Nothing like an evening with the Bard, I reasoned, to cool the Indian public's over-heated fantasies about our mass orgies.

Our theatre company had excellent English actors, some of whom had been professionals before dropping out and travelling to Pune. We made costumes in traditional *sannyas* colours – from yellow through orange to red – and injected truckloads of enthusiasm into the project. It was a great experience, travelling around India by bus and train, strutting and fretting our hour upon the stage.

We did well in Pune, Mumbai and other cities, but, alas, we bombed in Delhi. The main reason was that I'd been given the task of choosing between a large auditorium and a small, intimate theatre for the play's venue. So many people seemed interested in coming that I chose the auditorium, but failed to hire a sound system to amplify our voices – there were no radio mics in those days. As a result, only about a quarter of the audience could hear our lines and the capital's newspapers, eager to prove their cultural superiority over a bunch of foreigners, gleefully shredded us.

So, having learned a bruising lesson, the projected size of Osho Arts Festival audience didn't make sense. It wasn't a deal breaker, this early in the game, but it bothered me.

As a first step towards Delhi, I agreed to meet Ragni, a young Indian woman with showbiz links in Bollywood who – so I was told – would make a video of the play, while it was being performed. We met over coffee at Dario's, a chic Italian restaurant next door to the resort. Ragni walked in half-an-hour late, wearing a casually elegant blouse and matching pants, her designer sunglasses pushed back on top of her head, her long black hair falling down over her shoulders.

 Anand Subhuti

She weaved her way elegantly through the tables towards me, waving a friendly 'hello' while talking with cool efficiency into her shiny, white Samsung Galaxy. Jackie Kennedy herself couldn't have made a better entrance.

We shook hands, ordered cappuccino and pretty soon she was offering me good news and bad news.

"I like your script and I want to be involved," she told me, having read the copy I'd emailed to her. This, of course, was the good news.

"But to be honest with you, I don't think this festival is going to happen," Ragni confided bluntly. "The organiser keeps shifting his venues and dates. I don't think he's got his act together."

Reluctantly, I had to agree with her. I'd gotten a similar message from a friend of mine called Chinmaya, an English-born musician who'd also been invited to perform at the festival. An inveterate hippie, Chinmaya had the distinction of playing at Paul McCartney's marriage to Heather Mills at a castle in Ireland in 2002.

McCartney had been impressed with Chinmaya's album *Celtic Ragas*, released one year earlier, in which my friend, playing his sarod – a stringed instrument half-way between a guitar and a sitar – had transformed Celtic ballads into classical Indian music. Since the ageing Beatle was willing to spend £3 million on the wedding, he happily paid for Chinmaya and his band to perform.

It was difficult to reassemble the band of musicians who'd accompanied Chinmaya on the recording of *Celtic Ragas*, because, as sannyasins tend to do, they'd already scattered across the planet. But back they came and yes, on that fateful day in June 2002, in the grounds of a remote castle in Glaslough, Ireland, Paul and Heather stood before Chinmaya's band while they played their Anglo-Indian mix.

That, of course, was the high point of Paul and Heather's ill-fated marriage. All too soon, she realized she could never replace McCartney's first wife, Linda, in the Beatle's wounded heart. All too soon, he understood that this woman was no submissive, fawning geisha, awed by his name and fame, but an untameable lioness with a full set of fangs. Their love affair died almost as quickly as the band dispersed after the gig.

Eleven years later, Chinmaya told me he'd agreed to participate in the proposed Delhi Arts Festival, but was forced to withdraw when no money was provided for him to book and retain other band members. McCartney could pay up front. Our man in Delhi could not.

"I'm afraid the organizer's a dreamer; he's all hot air," Chinmaya added.

The festival was disappearing, but a new friendship was forming. Ragni and I liked each other. To me, she was attractive, intelligent and extremely capable, with just a touch of steel beneath her soft exterior. She was 28 years old, about to produce her first movie in Mumbai and had her own production company.

We got along well for three reasons: we both loved show business, we both liked new creative projects and we were both sannyasins. Oh yes, and we both wanted to put on the play as quickly as possible, if not in Delhi, then in Mumbai; if not in Mumbai, then in Pune.

Mumbai seemed too expensive so we opted for a two-night-run in an old, dilapidated Pune theatre that was so funky it was hilarious. The stage had no wings, there were no lighting bars and no sound system. Everything had to be rented from outside.

One poor guy, who'd waited all afternoon to buy a ticket, came to Ragni just before curtain-up to complain that the back of his seat was missing. He had nothing on which to lean while watching the show! The place was like that, falling apart, as if nothing had been done to it since the departure of the Raj.

Also, I have to admit, the actors weren't really up to par. They did their best, but we had no time to recruit talent. So Hamlet turned out to be a young Indian guy with a broad Australian accent (he lived in Melbourne) who was far too cheerful to hold down the role, while Ophelia was a last-minute discovery: an English backpacker who happened to be staying in the same guest house as myself and who, as a starry-eyed teenager, had once dreamed of playing Ophelia.

"I'll play the part if you let me keep the wig and costume afterwards," she bargained.

It was an offer I couldn't refuse.

"Deal."

The show went ahead. We got away with it, but I knew we could do better.

Twelve months later, we'd shifted from the worst theatre in town to one of the best: an open-air amphitheatre with seating for 650 people, surrounded by a shopping mall that shielded it from traffic noise. When the sun went down and the lights were turned on, the place looked magical.

It was outrageously expensive by local standards, costing US $2000 per night, which was completely bizarre because few people could afford it, so most of the time it was unused, looking forlorn and abandoned. Moreover, the wooden floor, exposed to an annual cycle of ferocious heat and continuous rains, was so little used that it became too rough for actors to walk on without hurting their feet.

Over the years, efforts had been made to persuade the owner of the shopping mall to lower the rental price, but she wouldn't budge. She didn't need to. Her husband was the owner of some huge petro-chemical conglomerate and I suspect he gave her the mall as a plaything to keep her occupied.

She did, however, give us a cheaper deal for the second night, so we could just about afford to put on our play for two consecutive evenings.

It was a great venue, but intimidating. When I first walked out onto that stage, one sunny afternoon, a couple of weeks before showtime, my stomach knotted up in fear. It was one massive, circular, empty podium. To give you an idea: the London Palladium, arguably Britain's most famous theatre, has a stage that's 12 metres across, which caters to an audience of 2,286 people. This one, constructed in some obscure shopping mall and virtually unknown – even in Pune – was over 16 metres. How could we, a small, disparate group of amateur actors and actresses, create a convincing dramatic atmosphere on this oversized pill?

The stage came stark naked, with no frills attached, so again we had to hire everything: a generator to supply power, a lighting system, radio mics, amplifiers and speakers, a huge set to cover the width of the stage, plus a vast expanse of jute hessian matting to cover the rough floorboards.

The costs kept mounting. I had some great sponsors, including wealthy sannyasin friends who handed over generous amounts of cash, but the bills kept coming and in the end I had to dig into my own pockets.

     Anand Subhuti

However, there is one handsome bonus that India offers to theatrical entrepreneurs like myself: cheap fabrics and cheap tailoring, so we were able to create beautiful costumes for the play. All the guys would wear doublets, a kind of cross between a shirt and a jacket, and below the waist they wore breeches, which were... well, kind of puffy, inflated shorts, much in demand by Elizabethan gentlemen to show off their stocking-sheathed legs.

But we drew the line at showing off the crotch. This, may I remind you, was done with codpieces, those strange pouches attached to the front of men's trousers in medieval times to either accentuate their potency, or to conceal the fact that their genitals were swollen and rotting from syphilis, which, so some historians claim, was rampant in Europe at the time.

Since genitals were not highlighted in the script, we deemed codpieces an unnecessary distraction. In any case, I didn't want to risk the kind of 'wardrobe malfunction' – to borrow phrase immortalized by Janet Jackson – that would occur if one fell off.

The women, of course, wore long dresses, with long sleeves, befitting the modesty of the era. Mrs Shakespeare had a lovely green gown, Ophelia had her dreamy, creamy, diaphanous dress, but the real eye-catcher was Queen Elizabeth's dazzling, all-gold, shoulder-to-ankle outfit, made of a silky, shiny fabric that we found while shopping in downtown Pune.

Really, India has so many fabrics at affordable prices that it's a designer's paradise. And we had a lucky break: we found a tailor, close to the ashram, who was probably the only one in Pune who'd studied Elizabethan costumes as part of her education. When we showed her photos of our characters, culled from Google Images and hastily printed on A4 paper, she nodded and said "Yes, I can do it."

Her name was Ritu, she was in her late thirties and she earned her bread and butter by making maroon robes for the Osho Resort – everyone visiting the ashram had to wear these plain, anonymous robes as part of the experience.

But Ritu had a serious problem creating Elizabeth's ruff – that stiff, white, peacock-style fan of delicate white lace that is shown on almost all portraits of the Virgin Queen. Our version of the ruff just wouldn't stay up. I guess, in the old days, they used some kind of whalebone frame, sitting on the queen's shoulders, but 400 years later, in deepest India, we found ourselves short of whales.

In despair, after many failed attempts, Ritu told me the only way to keep the ruff erect would be to tie it to the Queen's hair, at the back of her neck. I was okay with it, but we hit a roadblock: my English lady friend refused to contemplate it. In the end, we decided to let it flop.

The secret of Elizabethan ruffs had eluded us.

One more thing about the Queen's attire: in the early scenes of the play she wore a gold mask around her eyes. It made her look more menacing, but that wasn't the point. The mask symbolized her personality and, more universally, the social masks we all wear, all the time. And yes, that does include you and me.

Anand Subhuti

Chapter Eight

Our Royal Jailers

*H*amlet's dead father irritates me. What did he think he was doing? Coming back as a ghost, walking the castle at night, scaring everybody and then driving his son crazy by revealing he'd been murdered by his own brother, the new king, who'd also married his ex.

Everything was going just fine until he showed up. His former wife, Gertrude, seemed happy enough with her new husband, King Claudius. True, Hamlet was in a bit of a dark mood, following his father's unexpected demise, but he was sincerely in love with the beautiful Ophelia – and she with him – so one got the feeling he would soon snap out of it.

Moreover, Hamlet was going to rule the country, sooner or later. Providing Claudius and Gertrude produced no children to complicate the issue of succession, Hamlet would eventually wear the Danish crown. No problem. Situation sorted.

But, oh no. This miserable ghost had to come and spoil the party. I grant you, it's not very nice to have poison poured into your ear by your brother – or, indeed, by anybody – while you're asleep, thereby being deprived of your mortal coil, but once it's done you may as well get used to it.

If I'd been a Danish political reporter in Elsinore Castle after all the main characters in Shakespeare's play had been killed, I would have interviewed the ghost and asked him: "Are you happy now? Now that your son is dead? Now that the woman you once loved is dead? Now that your brother is dead? Now that *everybody* is dead? Do you have any comment for the obituary column of *The Disembodied Times?*"

I'd like to have heard his answer. But Shakespeare doesn't deal with that, which is odd because, when all the bodies are lying on the ground at the end of the play, one might, at the very least, expect the ghost to make one last appearance and say to his slain son "Job done, Hamlet. Good boy!" The two ghosts could've walked off, arm in arm.

This is one of the reasons why, in the mid-1970s, Osho became the first Indian mystic to introduce therapy groups in his ashram. Don't see the connection? Look at it this way: Hamlet needed therapy. Why? Because he wasn't free of his father's grip. He was ordered to take revenge and he obeyed like any frightened little child.

The only alternative he could imagine was to kill himself, hence his epic speech "To be or not to be..." It was good poetry but poor philosophy. It did not occur to Hamlet, at any time, to rebel against his father. There was no room to manoeuvre outside his narrow psychological box, unless you include the possibility of going mad.

I can't easily forgive the Bard for giving Hamlet such a claustrophobic view of life. After all, Will himself was familiar with the fallibility of fathers, having witnessed the phenomenon at first hand in the form of his own dad – John Shakespeare.

John was an upwardly mobile glover and leather worker in Stratford-upon-Avon, whose fortunes prospered so much that he rose to become the town mayor. Then he fell on hard times. My school books told me it was for 'unknown reasons'.

Ha! What rubbish! Were these teachers trying to protect their precious Shakespeare by concealing facts about his unscrupulous father? The truth is, John got busted for smuggling wool to avoid government taxes, a hugely lucrative but highly illegal business in Elizabethan times. That's why his fortunes crashed and his poor wife, Mary Arden, had to sell off her property just to keep the family afloat.

The ageing couple, John and Mary, lived for years in poverty until their genius son exploded into stardom on the London stage and basically took care of them for the rest of their lives. He even bought a coat of arms, restoring respectability to the Shakespeare name.

You'd think Will's willingness to rescue his own father would have allowed him to paint Hamlet with a broader brush. Surely, our luckless hero didn't need to be so obedient, so acquiescent, instantly agreeing to take on his dead dad's lust for revenge?

I have to concede, however, that the theme of obedience to one's elders continues to be relevant, even today, especially in royal families. I remember a remark made by Prince William, a couple of decades back, when he was about eleven years old. At the time, he must have been feeling uneasy about the pressure on him, as a future British monarch, attending weekly meetings with his grandmother to discuss royal duties, plus having to deal with his younger brother Harry's envy and resentment at being left out.

In a moment of unscheduled honesty, Wills remarked to Charles, his father, "Actually, I'd just as soon *not* be King."

We don't hear anything about that from Wills these days. Any hint of personal preference on such matters has been thoroughly suppressed, and with a grandmother like that sitting on his head, I'm really not surprised.

One more royal anecdote: back in the 1980s, soon after Charles and Diana were married, they were sitting with the Queen at a public event when the band struck up the national anthem. As the music played, Charles, in a rare moment of spontaneity and playfulness, leaned over to his young bride and whispered, "Darling, they're playing our tune."

Diana giggled a little too loudly, whereupon the Queen slowly turned her head and administered what the newspapers afterwards described as 'a killing stare' to her son and his wife. It shut them up in a second.

I've been on the receiving end of that stare myself, when I was a political correspondent. MPs from the Commons had been invited to Westminster Hall, close to the House of Lords, to congratulate the Queen on one of her anniversaries – she's had so many I've forgotten which. Most probably, it was her 25th year as Queen. Anyway, we 'Lobby Correspondents' came along to watch the show and report the event, standing high above, in the gallery.

A fanfare of trumpets announced the Queen's arrival, whereupon one of the MPs shouted, "Three cheers for her Majesty!" The sequence of 'hip-hip-hoorays' that followed

     Anand Subhuti

was, without doubt, one of the phoniest demonstrations of good cheer I have ever witnessed.

Then the Queen, Prince Philip, Charles and the rest of the Royals walked slowly through the hall towards the exit beneath us. The Queen raised her head and allowed her hostile, unforgiving eyes to rest upon the media whom, of course, she both hated and needed, just like all the politicians behind her. I felt a strong impulse to wave a hand, or at least give her a smile, but I knew would cost me my job, so I just stared back and declined to bow my head in loyal subjugation.

I don't want to give the Queen a hard time, but the truth is she acts as society's chief jailer, the ultimate role model, keeping us all safely locked inside the prison of correct social behaviour. And what, you may ask, is wrong with *correct social behaviour?* Well, nothing. Except it kills you. It shrivels your life energy to the point when you may as well be dead.

Osho created therapy groups to help us break loose from those psychological and emotional prisons – prisons built with lots of good intentions by mum and dad, not to mention schoolteachers, university professors, members of the clergy... and my own favourite role models: stiff, formal, well-spoken BBC television newscasters.

To me, watching TV back in the 60s, they looked so incredibly cool, talking about the chaos of world events without a flicker of emotion:

"Good evening, here is the news. Famine in Ethiopia has killed at least half a million people according to a report published today by the World Health Organization..." etc, etc.

As a young man, I wanted to be like them: professional observers of life, totally in control, untouched by anything faintly resembling human feelings. Maybe that was my motivation for becoming a journalist and also why, a few years later, I fell in love with the meditative image of Gautam Buddha.

Siddhartha's blissfully enlightened state, sitting cross-legged with a permanent smile on his face and a golden halo around his head, seemed like the ultimate escape from the ordinary ups and downs of human emotions. He was out of it. Safe. Beyond reach.

So you can imagine my alarm when I discovered that Osho encouraged us to go *into* our emotions. He wanted us to feel *more*, not less. He wanted us to take the lid off the pressure cooker of self-control that had been steadily building up steam since mom and dad first said "Be quiet! Don't pick your nose! Don't laugh, it's not funny! Big boys don't cry! Sit up straight..." and all the rest.

Osho invited us to *not* to keep it bottled up inside any longer. He wanted us to lose it – big time. Therapy with Osho was fun, exciting and scary. We had lots of emotional baggage to unload. We needed to scream, we needed to cry, we needed to shout and laugh and go nuts; we needed to dance around naked, hug each other, roll on the floor... feeling for the first time what it was like to be free of all restraint.

I remember one amazingly liberating moment when we were all naked, lying on our backs on the floor of the group room in one big circle of bodies, playing with our sexual organs – okay, call it 'masturbating' if you like – laughing and waving to our imagined parents, saying "Hi mom! Hi dad!"

Somehow I can't imagine Prince William doing that, can you? Maybe Prince Harry on a trip to Las Vegas...

Returning to the irritating spectre of Hamlet's father's

     Anand Subhuti

ghost, it seems to me this apparition is symbolic. He's the voice of our internalized morality, of all our 'shoulds' and 'should nots', of all the things we ought be doing – or not doing – if we wish to be recognized as good, obedient members of society.

In the UK, of course, the ultimate reward for this dutiful attitude is to receive a knighthood or some other decoration from the reigning monarch. And it's never too late to repent and rejoin the mainstream, because even a lost sheep can return to the cosy safety of the establishment fold.

Thus it was, on December 12, 2003, Michael Philip Jagger, after more than 40 years of sneering, hip-gyrating, rebellious rock 'n' roll, after decades of terrifying parents with sexualized songs that invited young people everywhere to cut loose from moral restraint, arrived at Buckingham Palace, came in from the cold and bowed down before the royal presence to receive his knighthood. The Queen couldn't bring herself to present the award to Jagger personally, so it was left to Charles, Prince of Wales, to do the deed.

Arise, Sir Mick.

"Have you seen your mother, baby, standing in the shadows..."

Actually, it wasn't your mother, Mick. It was the ghost of Hamlet's father.

Chapter Nine

The Prince Must Die

*H*amlet is smiling. That's odd. I don't recall any point in the Bard's tale when Hamlet is cheerful. But maybe it's because my version of the play is a little different and this young man has just watched his girlfriend, Ophelia, strip off her courtly gown and dance around the stage as Lady Raga, wearing little more than a pair of sunglasses.

As a playwright in urgent need of gloom and doom, Will must put a stop to this.

"Hey, what are you smiling at?" he enquires icily, getting up from his seat and crossing the stage towards him.

Hamlet, still distracted, beams at Will with a stupid grin on his face, and says, "She's kinda cute, isn't she?"

Ruled, as all young men are, by their surging hormones, Hamlet has forgotten all about sending Ophelia to a nunnery. Testosterone seems to have triumphed.

"Young man, I am a genius in the use of English language and the word 'cute' does not appear in any of my plays," Will curtly informs him. "Ophelia is a tragic figure, doomed to drown in a lake."

     Anand Subhuti

He takes Hamlet by the arm and brings him downstage towards the audience.

"Now then, the big question is: how should you die?"

The smile disappears from Hamlet's visage – that's better. Let's have little respect for the impending disaster that is about to descend on the luckless pair.

"Do I have to, Will?" he asks, pleadingly.

It is Will's turn to be cheerful, slapping Hamlet on the back as if it's the most natural thing in the world. "Of course, man. How can *Hamlet* be a tragedy if you don't die?"

Turning towards the wings on the right side of the stage, he calls out loudly, "Where are the instruments of death?" Immediately, an attendant comes walking towards him, bearing a tray that carries a wine cup, a bottle of poison, an old flintlock pistol and two swords.

Which is it to be? Let's go for poison, since it's already a dominant theme in this tragedy. Warming to his task, Will picks up the bottle, then shakes a few drops of poison into the wine cup, telling Hamlet, "Now, suppose the new king pours a glass of wine, sprinkles poison in it, then offers it to you to drink?"

Hamlet reluctantly accepts the cup, looks at the audience, winks, slowly brings it to his lips and then, at the very last moment, drops it on the floor. With a look of mock astonishment on his face that fools no one, he turns to Will and exclaims innocently, "Ooops! Sorry, I dropped it."

Slightly irritated but undeterred, Shakespeare picks up the old flintlock pistol and hands it to him: "Or, perhaps, in your despair, you put a pistol to your head and pull the trigger..."

Historically speaking, I'm not sure whether this type of pistol was available in Elizabethan England. I fancy it was invented much later, but some dramatic licence is needed – I can't think of other convenient ways to kill off this guy.

Again, with extreme reluctance, Hamlet slowly brings the muzzle of this weapon to the side of his head. Closing his eyes tightly and grimacing with anticipated pain, he squeezes the trigger and there is a sharp "click," but no report, no sound of a gunshot.

Looking surprised and relieved, Hamlet inspects the weapon then says to Shakespeare smugly, "Will, you forgot to load it!"

At this point, Will has reason to become extremely upset, but another idea has already entered his fertile head and he immediately jumps on it.

"I have it! Hamlet must die in a sword fight..." He grabs the two swords from the tray and offers one, handle first, to the doomed young man in front of him.

"Come on man, take one of these and defend yourself."

Gingerly, Hamlet takes the sword while Will poses like one of the *Three Musketeers*, his blade outstretched at arms length, ready for some scintillating swordplay. But his opponent delays, engaging the audience in a series of theatrical asides while trying to figure a way out of the situation.

"My god, do I really have to fight?" he ponders nervously. Inspiration dawns in the form of a time warp that allows him to mimic one of Hollywood's hardest, meanest showdown specialists.

"Maybe I can scare him with my Clint Eastwood impersonation," Hamlet conjectures, then squinting in supercool fashion through half-closed eyelids, he looks at me and drawls slowly, "Go ahead, make my day."

Who does this young man think he's trying to impress?

"You can't threaten me, I'm a master swordsman," Will scoffs, making a couple of passes in front of him with a swish and flourish.

Hamlet persists with his teeth-grinding, menacing tone, "Will, you've got to ask yourself one question, 'Do I feel lucky? Well, do ya, punk?'" He's really doing a good impression of Eastwood. But now Will has had enough.

"Where are you getting these cheap Hollywood lines from? Fight man, fight!"

Hamlet shrugs in a gesture of resignation and confides to the audience, "When all else fails... Arnold Schwarzenegger..." Turning towards the Bard he suddenly charges at him with alarming ferocity crying, "Hasta la vista baby!"

Will is taken by surprise and is beaten back by Hamlet's oncoming fury. He doesn't have a chance to use his skill, he's too busy defending himself. Staggering backwards, he can't see where he's going, trips and falls. Hamlet stands over him, the tip of his sword pointing directly at Shakespeare's heart.

Now it's Will's turn to seek inspiration and, remembering that he is, after all, the one writing the play, he raises a hand and exclaims, "Wait! Wait! I forgot. There must be treachery involved."

He calls to the attendant who is still holding the tray: "Give me that bottle of poison!" Pulling out the cork, he carefully allows a few drips to stain the edge of his blade.

"Your enemy has put poison on the tip of his sword," he informs Hamlet. "One small cut and all is lost..."

In act of ungentlemanly subterfuge, he then points across the stage, behind Hamlet, with his free hand saying, "Look over there!"

Poor Hamlet. The innocent young man turns to look where Will is pointing and the cowardly Bard stabs him in the thigh. Immediately, the poison takes effect and Hamlet groans and staggers across the stage in a classic dying scene pulled from any ancient black-and-white Western movie in which the bad guy has been shot. After many moans and groans, he finally collapses in a heap downstage right.

Will is unrepentant and immensely satisfied.

"That's much better," he announces, standing up and dusting himself off.

A fanfare of trumpets announces the impending arrival of royalty and, sure enough, Queen Elizabeth sweeps onto the stage.

"Where is our playwright, Master Shakespeare?" she enquires, looking above the heads of the audience as if she cannot see the Bard humbly bowing before her. This is an effective strategy used by people in power since time immemorial. They act as if they can't see you, or as if you aren't there, reminding you of your insignificant status.

Will must therefore attract her attention.

"Here, Your Majesty... your humble servant awaits your bidding."

"We are interested in the progress of your a new play," declares Good Queen Bess, allowing a faint touch of menace to be heard in her voice. She likes to keep Will on a short leash. She knows she can't trust artists or, come to think of it, anyone else in her court, or, indeed, in the entire country. Surrounded by conspiracies and enemies, her 45-year reign was a miracle of survival.

     Anand Subhuti

"Yes, Your Majesty, it's coming along nicely," says Will, fawningly. He's so obsequious, it's really quite disgusting.

"What is this drama to be called?" she enquires.

"Hamlet, Prince of Denmark, Your Majesty."

"Indeed? We are curious as to how you intend this play to end...," the supreme power pauses for a moment and then, ratching up the menace factor a notch or two, she asks, "In *tragedy*, we trust?"

Now here's a stroke of luck for Will, who, let's face it, could use a break. He's had a rough time trying to keep control of his play, but just at this particular moment there happens to be a dead body lying on the stage.

Pointing to the crumpled heap of flesh, Will nods and smiles, saying "Oh yes, indeed, ma'am. All the main characters die."

For a moment, her Royal Majesty allows her eyes to rest upon the heap, whose impressive lack of any signs of life indicates her wishes are being obeyed.

"Excellent," she pronounces. "Our people must be continuously reminded that life is filled with melancholy, suffering and death."

To Will's relief, the Royal presence turns away and exits whence she has come. Making sure the Queen has gone, the Bard gets off his knees and strolls over to Hamlet's prone form, nudging it with his foot.

"Arise, oh corpse!" he commands.

Surprised and puzzled, Hamlet raises his head to look at Shakespeare. "But I'm dead," he reminds the playwright.

Will shakes his head impatiently. "No, no. That was just a temporary death to keep Her Majesty the Queen off my back." He grabs Hamlet's hand and pulled him to his feet, then adds encouragingly, "Don't worry, you will die permanently, later in the play."

Hamlet rolls his eyes in disbelief.

"Gee, thanks Will!" he mutters and leaves the stage.

Pulling back from the action for a moment, one might enquire, at this point in the play, where the audience's affection lies. Obviously, with the lovers, Hamlet and Ophelia. They will want this youthful couple to avoid a dreadful fate. Also, with Mrs Shakespeare, because if anyone can navigate through these treacherous political waters and bring all the characters to safe harbour, it is she. And I'm pretty sure the audience has some sympathy with Will, caught as he is between the conflicting will-power – no pun intended – of two strong women.

If there is any kind of archetypal 'bad guy' it must be Queen Elizabeth, because she is the one driving the plot development towards tragedy. She has her excuses, being so old and friendless, but still, there's no need for her to take it out on others.

In any drama, you've got to have a bad guy to create tension and there's a peculiar thing about being bad: it's subject to the law of relativity. I don't know if Albert Einstein ever noticed, or applied his discovery to cinema dynamics, but good guys can also be bad, providing the bad guys are *really, really* bad.

In other words, the more evil the bad guy, the more nasty the good guy is allowed to be. That's how Clint Eastwood was able to triumph at the box office with his mean, tough, rule-breaking character, *Dirty Harry*, and other roles like him. The villains in these movies are so revoltingly psychotic, the hero can do pretty much what he likes in the way of being vicious.

Hasta la vista baby...

   Anand Subhuti

Our own villain, Queen Bess, is more straightforward in her approach – she simply wants everyone dead – so there is no need for so crude a hero as Mr Eastwood might provide.

If there is to be a happy ending, it is likely to come through ingenuity and inspiration, not through pointing a gun at someone and saying, "Ask yourself, 'Do I feel lucky?'"

Well, do ya, Will? 'Cos it sure looks like you're gonna need it.

Chapter Ten

So Great a Thing

I need to tell you how Shakespeare saved my life. It happened when I was working on a newspaper called *The Birmingham Post*, not as a political correspondent in London, but several months before that unexpected promotion was given to me. I was living in Birmingham itself, working at the newspaper's head office, tucked away in obscurity on the business desk, filing stories about local companies making ball-bearings and ashtrays for automobiles.

I hated Birmingham, which is really unfair because it was an important step on my road to journalistic success. Well, to give you the full picture, I'd better start from the beginning...

You see, after graduating from Bristol University with a degree in Politics and Philosophy, I was somewhat dismayed to realize I had to earn a living. My free ride had lasted three years – student grants didn't need to be repaid in those golden days – but in the end I had to step out into the big, wide, intimidating world and forge a career for myself.

My degree seemed useless. I was too intelligent to go

     Anand Subhuti

into politics and bored stiff by philosophy. But journalism looked attractive because writing came easily to me and it didn't feel like 'real work'. So I got a job as a cub reporter on a daily newspaper called the *Evening Advertiser*, published in an unremarkable little town called Swindon.

Mostly, it was boring stuff, like council meetings, but once in a while it was fun, such as the time I exposed a local factory for covering people's allotments and vegetable gardens with a dusting of deadly cyanide powder that was pouring out from its chimneys.

18 months into my new career, there was a problem. My girlfriend, graduating two years behind me at Bristol, had just completed her final exams for a law degree and wanted to spend the whole summer exploring the Greek islands.

I, on the other hand, was allowed only two weeks holiday. I asked the editor for an extra four weeks unpaid leave and was promptly refused. This left two options: lose my girlfriend or walk out the door, knowing I would not be allowed back.

I was scared. If I quit, it might destroy my career. But something in me rebelled against the idea of waiting until I retired at the age of 65 in order to enjoy life. Why should I be subjected to such economic slavery? Why should I sacrifice 'now' for the promise of a good time 'then'?

I quit. I collected my two weeks' holiday pay, received a bottle of whiskey as a parting gift from my disbelieving colleagues in the newsroom – they didn't think I would go through with it – and in a display of bravado told them, "By the time I've finished this bottle, I will have forgotten all about you, and you will have forgotten all about me."

I flew to Athens with my girlfriend. We took ferry boats around the islands... Paros, Naxos, Ios, Crete...We made love by moonlight on deserted beaches... We took horseback rides over mountains... We fought once in a while, got sunburned occasionally, but mostly had a good time.

Six weeks later, back in the UK, I put in a call to an old friend who'd also worked on the *Advertiser* in Swindon but was now a reporter on *The Birmingham Post*.

"Any jobs up your way, Des?" I asked him.

His reply astonished me. "Yes, mine. I'm off to study Russian at university for four years."

I wrote to his editor, was interviewed and got the job. I didn't say anything about breaking my contract with the *Evening Advertiser* and apparently my new editor saw no need to obtain references – thank god, because he wouldn't have got them.

Through this remarkable turn of events, I gained new understanding about the way life works, not just for me but for everyone. Life, I realised, is a different creature from the beast we're warned against by our parents, teachers and other well-wishers. Life, according to them, is dangerous. We're advised to be cautious, hard-working, obedient, looking for job security, pension rights, health insurance – trying to create as many safety nets as we can.

The spectre of living recklessly and then finding oneself huddled inside a cardboard box under Charing Cross Railway Bridge – like George Orewell in *Down and Out in Paris and London* – shivering with cold with only other poor bums for company, is a powerful image to inspire caution in us all.

What I discovered, however, was just the opposite. Life appreciates gamblers, people with guts, people willing to take risks. I'm not talking about stupid risks like putting your life-savings on a horse in the Grand National, or trying to swim the Atlantic Ocean without the lifejacket (or even with one). I'm talking about taking risks that help you lead a more fulfilling life.

Osho once said, "Existence always supports those in search of truth." In other words, life isn't something alien, hostile and antagonistic to you. It wants you to be courageous, independent and free.

I didn't understand this all at once, just by landing a job on *The Birmingham Post*. It came in installments, over the years. But it's always been true for me and I have the feeling it's true for everybody.

I was relieved to be employed as a journalist once more. But, all too soon, I realised that business reporting in Birmingham was a terribly dull affair. The motor industry dominated the West Midlands and this might have been an interesting gig, especially test-driving the latest cars, but the *Post* already had a special correspondent for everything moving on four wheels. I was confined to the ball-bearing, windshield wiper and ashtray department.

To give you an example, I was asked to write about a newly-invented emergency fan belt for cars. It was a handy device and I actually used it myself, after breaking down on the M1 motorway, but well... it wasn't exactly an epic story, was it? It didn't send shock waves of astonishment through our readers.

I had a vague feeling I was destined for greater things.

To save myself from increasing despair, I viewed the job as a temporary stepping stone. I had my eyes set on London and figured that, with a little luck, I could eventually make my way onto a national newspaper like *The Guardian* or *The Times*. With even more luck, I might eventually land a really interesting job like political reporting.

But then my girlfriend moved to London, rented a flat in trendy Muswell Hill, got herself a fun job at Thomson Holidays and promptly dumped me. Suddenly, I saw myself through her eyes: a third-rate journalist going nowhere, trapped in the Midlands, far from the action of Swinging London.

From then on, Birmingham became unbearable. Recalling my bold decision to leave the *Advertiser* and travel to Greece, I was ready to take new risks, but I couldn't figure out which way to jump. I felt increasingly suffocated, but with no clue how to change things.

Now comes the Bard to the rescue. One day, sitting in the office, I received word that a pub was going to open in South Birmingham, near the Bournville chocolate factory, owned by the Cadbury family. This sounds, on the face of it, a less than earth-shattering announcement. But it was much, much bigger than one might think.

The Cadbury family was deeply religious and, back in the 19th century, had looked after its workers far better than anyone else in England's industrial heartland. At a time when there were no unions, no minimum wage, no safeguards of any kind, the Cadburys were model employers, building whole neighbourhoods near their factories to provide housing for their workers, setting up schools to educate their kids...taking care of just about everything.

There was only one golden rule: No booze. No pubs. No alcohol. This rule had held for over 100 years, but now, as the family loosened its grip on the area, the first pub had finally appeared.

How to present the story? What came to me was a line from *Antony and Cleopatra*, which I'd studied at school. The

Anand Subhuti

play, as we all know, is a power struggle between Octavius Caesar and two passionate lovers, Antony and Cleopatra. Caesar wins a crucial battle and, rather than face surrender and humiliation, Anthony impales himself on his own sword.

Not to be upstaged, Cleopatra then picks up an asp, a poisonous snake, and allows it to bite her, ending her mortal existence. When I picture this scene, inevitably I think of Elizabeth Taylor, dressed all in gold, her cleavage well displayed even in death, lying on a white bier, at the end of the most expensive movie ever made (this was 1963). I was an 18 year-old teenager at the time and quite impressed, both by Taylor's cleavage and the movie's price tag.

Anyway, when Caesar hears of the deaths of Anthony and Cleopatra, he is astonished and declares:
`The breaking of so great a thing should make a bigger crack!`

Caesar imagines that, in keeping with such momentous news, there should be earthquakes, thunderstorms, lions walking in city streets... there should be great dramatic events as nature responded to these deaths.

So that was my headline, my intro to the Cadbury story:

The breaking of so great a thing should make a bigger crack! One hundred years of teetotal puritanism gone down the drain, shattered by a single pub.

The editor loved it. He thought it was marvellous. From then on, he appreciated me as a writer. So when, a few weeks later, his political reporter in London asked for an assistant to help with the workload at the Houses of Parliament, he fingered me for the job.

It was deliverance. A gift from the divine. Suddenly, out

of nowhere, I was freed. Not only that, I was promoted. Not only that, I was being asked to do political reporting – the very thing for which I'd been aiming, with many steps in between, further down the road.

There and then, I was ready to buy my train ticket to London. But the business editor, a dour Scotsman called Mac, had other ideas. Squinting at me from under his bushy eyebrows he grunted, "Well, ye canna goo til we've orl hud oor soomer holidees."

His roadblock stopped me in my tracks. Of course, he was right. The business desk had to be manned while its reporters took their vacations. In any case, Parliament was going into summer recess, so there was no need for two reporters until the annual party conferences in the autumn. But I couldn't wait. Another two months in Birmingham? Impossible. I had to get out... now.

I went to the editor. "It's going to take me a while to find an apartment in London and also to find my way around Westminster, learning the ropes," I explained. "Is it okay if I leave now?"

The editor had no problem with it. I returned to the business desk, saying nothing, and an hour later two white envelopes were delivered by the editor's secretary to Mac and myself. We opened them simultaneously. It was a directive from the editor that I would be leaving for London within the week.

I had a split second to find my way around Mac's wounded ego before he stormed into the editor's office to protest. Looking at him with as much gratitude as I could generate, I smiled thankfully and said, "Gosh, thanks Mac!" making it seem like he'd been the one to send me off.

It was an Academy Award-winning performance,

    Anand Subhuti

spontaneously scripted in a moment of urgent need. But would it work?

Mac hesitated, scrutinising my face for any sign of duplicity, then grunted "That's okay laddie" and let it pass. My love for the acting profession was born. Three days later, I was at New Street Station, boarding the train for King's Cross. So long Birmingham.

During my time at Westminster, I used Shakespeare quotes a couple more times as intros for news stories, but none of them worked as well as the first one.

However, there was something strange about the job itself, which I need to mention before ending this part of my tale. As far as I could see, there was absolutely no need for *The Birmingham Post* to have two men in Westminster. For a regional daily, this luxury didn't make sense. One man was more than enough.

If I'd been the editor, I'd have told the guy in London "You feel overworked? No problem. Just do what you can and we'll pick up the rest from the wire services."

But I wasn't about to argue. Offering silent prayers to some unknown deity, I stepped off the train at King's Cross, joined a couple of friends in an apartment near Marble Arch, bought myself some snappy Village Gate suits and headed for the House of Commons.

Thank you, Will Shakespeare. Thank you, God. Thank you, Colin Silk, the eccentric old English teacher at Lewes County Grammar School for Boys who introduced us to *Antony and Cleopatra*. Thank you, John Lewis, political correspondent for *The Birmingham Post*, who pleaded with the editor for an unnecessary assistant.

Why am I so grateful? Because, even though I was thrilled with my new job as a Lobby Correspondent, the excitement didn't last. Within two years, I was bored with British politics and wanted out. Not just out of Westminster, but out of the country, out of my made-in-the-UK personality and out of my mind.

I made it. But that's another story.

 Anand Subhuti

Chapter Eleven

The Story of the West

We are approaching that moment in the play where my wife, Mrs Shakespeare, single-handedly demolishes Western materialism. Or, rather, she puts it firmly in its place. Since I am the one who wrote the words she is about to utter, I must take responsibility and point out that I'm not against materialism. I like my laptop, mobile and refrigerator as much as the next guy.

But it's time for a reality check; time to see how smug and satisfied we are with living on the surface of human consciousness, surrounded by pleasant consumeristic distractions, not even considering the possibility of diving deeper.

As a loyal husband, I am required to support my wife, so I'm using the phrase 'single-handedly' rather loosely. The truth is, as the Bard, I'm not as convinced as Mrs Shakespeare about the shallowness of Western values, but once in a while a husband has to stand by his woman – or face the consequences.

As she comes on stage, I rise from my seat and together we address the audience. Mrs Shakespeare begins, "You seem like an intelligent group of people, so let me ask you a question. Don't you think it's odd that in the whole history of Western culture nobody knew anything about meditation?

Will: "All those European geniuses..."

Mrs: "French Impressionist painters..."

Will: "Russian novelists..."

Mrs: "Italian sculptors..."

Will: "German composers..."

There is a brief pause as I wait for my wife to realize there's an important omission in her list of Europe's most talented artists.

Mrs: "Oh yes, and not forgetting the English playwrights."

Will is relieved and gratified. "Thank you, dear," he murmurs, acknowledging his rightful place among the cultural elite.

Mrs: "And not one of them ever sat down, closed his eyes and meditated."

Will: "They knew everything about the human ego."

Mrs: "But they didn't know anything about dropping the ego."

Will: "They knew how to be *Somebody*."

Mrs: "But they had no idea how to be *Nobody*."

At this point, we move into a kind of poetic dialogue:

Mrs: "Don't you think it's kind of odd? Don't you think it's kind of strange?"

Will: "Such a funny situation, no one's heard of meditation."

Mrs: "If you say the world is maya..."

Will: "You will just be called a liar."

Mrs: "If you point towards nirvana..."

     Anand Subhuti

Will: "They will say you've gone bananas."
Mrs: "If you tell them not to think…"
Will: "They will send you to a shrink."
Mrs: "If you ask them to be still…"
Will: "They will offer you a pill."
Mrs: "If you talk of inner vision…"
Will: "They will think of television."
Mrs: "If you sit silently alone…"
Will: "Don't switch off your mobile phone."
Mrs: "If you want to clear your head…"
Will: "You can Google it instead."
Mrs: "If you want true happiness…"
Will: "Just send an SMS."
Mrs: "If you want to raise your spirit…"
Will: "Any shopping mall will do it."
Mrs: "You can find out who you are…"
Will: "At Manchester United Café Bar…"

I have to interrupt our repartee at this point and explain that in Pune one of the most chic places to be seen having coffee or drinking a beer is located in the city's most fashionable shopping mall, Amanora, which is packed with brand clothing, jewellery and every symbol of foreign fashion you can imagine. There, amid the Louis Vuitton handbags, Calvin Klein jeans, Victoria's Secret lingerie and Marks & Spencer socks, you find the Manchester United Cafe Bar, where you can buy expensive drinks and be seen watching big-screen reruns of England's most successful football club in action on the field. It's the height of cool, especially for men.

That's why I chose to include it in our diatribe against Western values. It also happens to be the only trendy cafe in Pune whose name rhymes nicely with "find out who you are." In Europe, I'd simply say "You can find out who you are, in your local pub or bar."

Now we can continue:

Mrs: "That's the story of the West."

Will: "There's no time to stop and rest."

Mrs: "Just to be..."

Will: "And let the rest..."

Mrs: "Disappear..."

Together: "In emptiness."

For a moment, we stand silently together with eyes closed, illustrating the inner state about which we speak. Then we turn to face each other, give a namasté greeting, and Mrs Shakespeare quietly leaves the stage.

I watch her go and then feel free to distance myself from what has just occurred, turning to the audience and saying "My wife's in love with Eastern philosophy. Oh, it's interesting, I grant you, but what can you do with it? It's not going to pay the rent is it? It's not going to get me out of trouble with the queen. So, it's back to work for me."

I have to say this, or the play would end right here. We would simply declare, *"Hey Ram! All is God! All is One! Duality is but an fleeting illusion created by an even more illusory Self!"* Thereafter, we would sit cross-legged on the stage, contemplating our navels, until the audience became bored and left. End of story, end of play, end of just about everything you can imagine.

But we're not done. The play must continue.

By the way, in case, you're thinking that my wife's speech is relevant only for the newly-enriched Indian bourgeoisie, may I remind you that almost everything in the UK is now branded. The corporate consumer culture has swallowed

   Anand Subhuti

us all and we happily wear their logos on our t-shirts, jeans, jackets, handbags, caps...

Brands are brashly displayed on the caps of racing drivers, the shirts of football players, the racquets of tennis champions and on the stadiums in which they perform. It gets worse every year. Soon they will be calling Westminster the Coca-Cola Commons and repackaging the Windsor franchise as the Ladbrokes Monarchy.

I can tell you one thing: if my grandfather had been told that he had to wear the name of his tailor on the outside of his jacket he would have shot himself. I kid you not. That's an indication of how far we've come in the last 50 years.

Okay, that concludes my rant about materialism. Now we can proceed with the story... Oh, I almost forgot... After these messages from my sponsors:

"This book is being written on a Lenovo laptop (*I went for a cheap deal on Amazon and have regretted it ever since*)... while I drink my morning Nescafe Gold (*I ran out of coffee beans and was desperate*)...after sending a quick SMS to my publisher on my Samsung Galaxy SIII Mini (*I couldn't afford an Iphone*) and eating a bowl of Kellog's Frosties (*sugar is really, really bad for you and your children*)... at my home in sunny Jutland (*ha!*) an ideal summer vacation spot for British holidaymakers (*you've got to be kidding... It's 13 degrees Celsius and pouring with rain outside my window right now, in the middle of June!!!*)..."

Chapter Twelve

Young Women, Old Men

Ophelia is not a happy thespian. She feels frustrated. She wants a bigger slice of dramatic action and I can't say I blame her. After her Lady Raga dance routine, she doesn't have many lines to speak, even though she's onstage for a big chunk of the time.

So I need to come up with a new idea. She's a young, good-looking blonde and I've just finished reading a book about the trials and tribulations of Marilyn Monroe as she attempted to forge an acting career for herself.

Typecast as a bimbo blonde, Marilyn struggled through many 'casting couch' situations, sometimes refusing the advances of producers and studio directors, but more often furthering her career giving them what they wanted: the chance to make love with a fantasy symbol of sex and glamour which they themselves had created out of a very ordinary young woman.

Thus inspired, I created a casting couch scene between William Shakespeare and Ophelia. Will is sitting in his chair at the side of the stage, as per usual, writing his tragic masterpiece, when Ophelia hesitantly approaches him.

     Anand Subhuti

Having tasted freedom as Lady Raga, she now envisions a different role for herself.

"Excuse me, Master Shakespeare," she says, timidly.

Will doesn't want to be disturbed and feels irritated by this intrusion.

"Yes, what is it now?" he snaps.

"I... I want to change my character," ventures Ophelia, not really believing she's got the guts to say this to the great playwright.

"You... what?" Will can't believe he's hearing this defiant whisper of rebellion from such an insignificant member of his acting troupe.

"I want to change my character," repeats Ophelia, more determinedly, gathering courage.

The Bard waves his quill pen in a dismissive gesture. "No, no. That's not going to happen. The play is almost finished."

Pleadingly, the young woman sinks down close to Will's chair, catching hold of his arm, begging him with her big innocent eyes.

"Please, sir! It's not much to ask, is it? I just want to live my own life. And you are such a clever genius, you can make anything possible."

Flattery will get you everywhere. Will stops writing, focuses attention on the beautiful girl in front of him and, in the time-honoured manner of every horny guy who ever found himself in a position of power over a helpless female, changes his tune. Suddenly, he's more accommodating, more friendly, more willing to listen.

Stroking Ophelia gently on the face and trying not to gaze too long at her heaving, emotion-filled bosom, he murmurs, "Hmm... You're a pretty little thing, aren't you? Listen, tomorrow my wife goes out of town to take care of her sick mother. Why don't you come to my house and we'll... talk about it... together... hmm?"

If it had been Monroe, she might have said yes. But Ophelia, innocent girl that she happens to be, isn't ready to accommodate the Bard's unbridled lust. She backs off to centre stage and addresses the audience thus:

"My god, this horny old goat is trying to seduce me! I've heard of the Hollywood casting couch, I've heard of the Bollywood casting couch, but I've never heard of an Elizabethan casting couch! Oh well, I guess it's always been the same. Right then..."

She adjusts her hair, as if looking in a mirror, makes her dress a little more tidy, puts on a winning smile and turns towards the Bard. Approaching him seductively, she brushes her hand lightly over his bald head, and, whispering in his ear, offers him this little poem:

> *Oh Master Shakespeare, you're such a handsome man*
> *And if you agree to help me, I'll give you what I can.*
> *Would you like to taste my cherry? It's so tender, it's so*
> *sweet!*
> *Would you like to squeeze my plums, while I'm lying at*
> *your feet?*
> *Shall I feed you some papaya, while we're lying on your*
> *bed?*
> *Or would my lover rather have... a twisted nose instead!*

Suddenly, she grabs hold of his nose and twists it violently, making the startled Bard cry out in pain.

"Ow! You hurt me, you little bitch!"

Ophelia shrinks back from his anger but is unrepentant, replying defiantly, "Well, you asked for it! You dirty old man!"

     Anand Subhuti

Will is enraged and points are condemning literary finger at the poor girl.

"You will regret this young lady. You will die before this play is done. Your fate is sealed!"

Ophelia gasps in shock, then sobs and sinks to the floor. Will sits back in his chair, nurses his aching nose for a few moments, then goes back to writing his play.

Here, I must pay my dues to Monroe, who inspired this scene with her account of how she once turned down the advances of a studio head in Hollywood. Monroe was asked to strip naked for the movie mogul in his office, which she did. At his direction, she bent over, but as he approached her, penis in hand, she declined his advances. Said Monroe, "I had never seen a man so angry". He banned her from his studio.

Monroe's career survived the experience and so, as it happens, does that of Ophelia. As she weeps in despair, Mrs Shakespeare comes to the rescue once more, gliding on from the wings, kneeling down next to Ophelia and tenderly stroking her arm.

At this moment, something rather bizarre happens. Mrs Shakespeare, slipping cosily into the role of a sympathetic friend, begins to sing a corny song titled *I've Never Been To Me* that, way back in 1982, became a one-hit wonder for a little known R&B singer called Charlene.

Sung by a 'woman of the world', the song is addressed to a desperate young wife and mother who would like to trade her mundane existence for the jet-set lifestyle the singer has led. The older woman describes how she has travelled the world, allowing herself to be seduced by wealthy, powerful men, but never found self-fulfillment. The basic message

to the younger woman is: be happy as a wife and mother –
that's the real thing.

To me, it's fascinating that Charlene, in her own life,
got to see both sides of the coin. When she first tried to
break into showbiz in the late 70s, signing on with Motown
Records, her songs – including *I've Never Been To Me* – never
reached higher than No. 97 in the charts.

So she gave up, married an Englishman, left the States
and descended into total obscurity, working in a sweet
shop in a tiny English town called Ilford.

Then, in 1982, at the urging of his girlfriend, a Florida
DJ started playing *I've Never Been To Me* and it rose from
the ashes to become a classic sleeper hit, reaching No. 3 in
the *Billboard* Hot 100 and becoming a global sensation. For
a moment, it seemed that a new career was being launched
for Charlene, but she had no further success and was never
able to convert that one hit into a singing career.

My problem with the song was that it almost fitted the
storyline, but not quite. The declaration *I've Never Been
To Me* parallels the realization of a spiritual seeker who
is just beginning to discover his, or her, inner world. But
Charlene's predictable, wholesome message of placing family
values above the jet-set lifestyle is offtrack, because when
you become interested in meditation you don't necessarily
change your way of living. Wife, mother, businesswoman,
movie star, international escort... the external role you play
in life is irrelevant to the inner journey.

Which is not to say that changes don't happen. For
example, Meera, India's most famous enlightened female
mystic, was a beautiful Rajput princess, belonging to a
royal family in Rajasthan, around 1500 AD. She became a
devotee of Krishna and then – to the horror of her family

     Anand Subhuti

– wandered the streets, singing and dancing in public, completely uninterested in her status as a princess.

But Charlene isn't singing about the kinds of changes that arise from spiritual transformation. She's simply moralizing in favour of staying home and being a good wife and mother rather than seeking adventure in the big wide world.

To make Charlene's song more relevant, I changed the hook line from *I've Never Been To Me* to a more positive assertion pointing in the same direction: *I'd Rather Be With Me*. I also changed the lyrics.

It's worth presenting the original lyrics and the new version in full, because it shows the essential difference between 'normal' values and the perspective of a seeker.

Here are Charlene's verses:

> *Hey lady, you lady, cursing at your life,*
> *You're a discontented mother and a regimented wife,*
> *I've no doubt you dream about*
> *The things you'll never do,*
> *But I wish someone had to talked to me*
> *Like I wanna talk to you.*
> *I've been to Georgia and California*
> *And anywhere I could run,*
> *Took the hand of a preacher man*
> *And we made love in the sun,*
> *But I ran out of places and friendly faces*
> *Because I had to be free,*
> *I've been to paradise, but I've never been to me*
>
> *Please lady, please lady, don't just walk away*
> *'Cause I have this need to tell you*
> *Why I'm all alone today.*

I can see so much of me
Still living in your eyes,
Won't you share a part of a weary heart
That has lived million lies

Oh I've been to Nice and the Isle of Greece
Where I sipped champagne on a yacht,
I moved like Harlowe in Monte Carlo
And showed 'em what I've got.
I've been undressed by kings
And I've seen some things
That a woman ain't supposed to see,
Hey lady, I've been to paradise
But I've never been to me.

Sometimes I've been to cryin' for unborn children
That might have made me complete,
But I took the sweet life and never knew
The bitter from the sweet.
I spent my life exploring the subtle whoring
That cost too much to be free,
Hey lady, I've been to paradise
but I've never been to me.

And here is the version I asked Mrs Shakespeare to sing to Ophelia:

Hey lady, young lady, weeping at your life,
You want to be a princess and you want to be a wife.
I can see you long to be
His sweet beloved one
And I hope for you that your dreams come true,
Now your life has just begun.
I've searched and roamed many miles from home

     Anand Subhuti

Looking for that special one,
Enjoyed a fling with a foreign king
And we made love in the sun.
I met Will and I love him still
And yet I want to be free
I've been around the world
But I'd rather be with me

Hey lady, dear lady, you will have your day
From my heart I want to tell you
That everything's okay.
I can see your destiny
Reflected in your eyes
You won't be apart and your open heart
Can see through all the lies.

It's strange but true, and I'm telling you
That nothing ever lasts.
The future will be present
And the present will be past.
Now the hardest thing is to look within
And find the real me
I've been around the world
But I'd rather be with me.

Mrs Shakespeare did well, lifting Ophelia out of her misery with this reassuring ballad, reviving her spirits after her shocking encounter with the sleazy Bard. Rounding the whole thing off by taking the younger woman by the hand, Mrs Shakespeare offers her a classic English solution to any personal difficulty:

"Come on, dear, let's have a cup of tea together".

They exit, arm in arm, two sisters brought together

by their mutual determination to survive Shakespeare's message of gloom and doom.

But, again, if this show ever takes off and goes commercial, we will have a serious copyright problem and be forced to pay large sums of unavailable funds to Charlene, wherever she is to be found – in an LA recording studio or back in a UK sweetshop.

Or, more likely, the Ravi-Subhuti team will need to create a new song that does the same job.

Anand Subhuti

Chapter Thirteen

Lady Macbeth

First Witch
When shall we three meet again, in thunder,
lightning, or in rain?

Second Witch
When the hurlyburly's done, when the battle's
lost and won.

Third Witch
That will be ere the set of sun...

$\mathcal{M}$y version of *Macbeth* is short. So short, in fact, that I can guarantee it will be never performed onstage. Not surprising, really, because there is zero suspense and therefore nothing to grip the audience.

You will recall that Macbeth, who in the opening scene fought so valiantly for King Duncan on the battlefield, is walking home with Banquo when he encounters three witches on the heath, who greet him thus:

First Witch: "All hail, Macbeth! Hail to thee, Thane of Glamis!"

Second Witch: "All hail, Macbeth! Hail to thee, Thane of Cawdor!"

Third Witch: "All hail, Macbeth! Thou shalt be king hereafter!"

The prophecy has been made. Macbeth goes home and tells his wife, the notorious Lady Macbeth, and she eagerly feeds his ambitious dreams, helping him plot the murder of the king that very night as he sleeps in their castle.

But in my version of the play, in the middle of their plotting and scheming, Macbeth suddenly laughs, scoops up his wife in his arms, whirls her around and declares:

> *Such fools are we, to hatch a plot like this*
> *When we can be transported into bliss.*
> *For if the witches prophecy be true*
> *There's really nothing for us both to do.*
> *It will happen by itself, you see,*
> *A murderer, I just don't need to be!*

Macbeth has a point. Either the prophecy is true, or it is not. If true, why should he do anything? Why should he try to make it happen? He can just relax, sip his favourite Scotch whiskey, eat a plate of haggis, listen to the wailing of his castle bagpipes and wait for events to overtake him.

No illusory daggers for Macbeth to clutch at, in his guilt and shame. No "Out damned spot!" for Lady Macbeth to scream at, in her madness and remorse. On the contrary, they can sit back and let it all unfold: Duncan accidentally chokes on a bowl of Scott's Porridge Oats, Banquo has a heart attack when Rangers beat Celtic, and the Macbeths are graciously invited to share Scotland's throne. End of story and curtain down.

But Will Shakespeare wasn't an idiot and he understood human nature. He knew that a certain human weakness

 Anand Subhuti

called 'lust for power' lies as a dormant seed within each and every one of us. All it lacks is opportunity. If such an opportunity presents itself, the hunger for power awakens and consumes us – and anyone else who stands in its path. This is the human frailty he portrays in *Macbeth*.

A few hundred years after Shakespeare died, Lord Acton declared:

Power corrupts. Absolute power corrupts absolutely.

Osho disagreed with the noble aristocrat. Power does not corrupt, he explained to us on many occasions. The corruption already exists within us but, most of the time, lacks the opportunity to manifest. Power simply allows whatever is unmanifest to show itself.

So allow me to set aside *Hamlet* for a moment and talk about the woman in my life who reminded me most of Lady Macbeth and her appetite for power. Normally, I wouldn't bother because we all know such people –- men and women – who succumb to ambition, as we ourselves are sometimes prone to do.

We've all been there... right? Even if it's only a question of organizing a village fete, chairing a council meeting, or managing the local Sainsbury's supermarket, we've all tasted power and found good, solid reasons why things need to be done *our* way and to hell with everyone else. So we're not exactly treading on fresh ground here.

Moreover, to talk about this, I have to go back more than 30 years and dig deep into my ageing memory banks, extracting details of events that are long gone. So, what's the point?

Well, in a truly extraordinary coincidence, those events came back to haunt the production of my play in Pune, disposing of half my audience. Overnight, about 500 people, who'd stated their intention to come to the show, simply failed to turn up.

This is how it happened:

Back in the 70s, as I've already mentioned, Osho's Pune ashram was a magnet for young Westerners and was highly controversial, making headlines through its free-sex image and no-holds-barred therapy groups in which people were screaming, fighting, fucking and generally letting it all hang out.

At the time, Osho was running the ashram through his Indian secretary, Laxmi, a tiny woman from Gujarat with fiery eyes and a brilliant, toothpaste-commercial smile. She, in turn, had her own secretary, a younger Indian woman called Sheela.

Since the ashram was much too small to handle the surging influx of Westerners, Osho asked Laxmi to find a bigger place in India. When she failed, Sheela nudged Laxmi aside and invited Osho to the USA, using donations from wealthy sannyasins to buy a 120-square-mile former cattle ranch in Oregon.

The fact that Osho went into silence – shortly before the Atlantic crossing – doubled Sheela's importance, because she also became the mystic's mouthpiece as well as his gofer.

Abrasive, rude and with a real talent to kick ass, Sheela ran the ranch for Osho, while we, his willing sannyasins, built an entire town for us all to live in, including houses, roads, power lines, reservoirs, sewage treatment plants... the works. It even had its own truck farm, dairy herd, bakery and enough henhouses to keep us supplied with omelettes... Oh yes, and a shopping mall, bar and casino. It was, if I say so myself, a phenomenal achievement.

Four years after our arrival, Sheela surprised us all by walking out and badmouthing Osho. She accused him of being more interested in collecting Rolls Royces – he had 93 by that time – than in caring for us, shaping an image of herself as the caring 'mother' of our community while Osho played with his fancy toys.

I'm not going to tell the whole story, because I've already done so, in a book about those years with Osho, titled, appropriately enough, *My Dance with a Madman*. Suffice to say that, after leaving Osho, Sheela wrote her own book, which was eventually published in Germany, while the rest of the publishing world yawned and declined her offering.

A great deal of water went down the Ganges and then, in 2013, almost thirty years after Sheela broke with the mystic – and 23 years after his death – her book was finally published in India. And guess what? It was published three days before the performance of our play.

Her book had quite an impact. The Indian media wasn't much interested in the Oregon end of her story. Instead, they jumped on her lurid tales about the Pune ashram, in which she emphasized free sex, unhygienic conditions, illness and especially the proliferation of STDs – sexually transmitted diseases. Really, the way she told it, the place sounded awful. The love we shared and the silence we experienced in meditation were both missing from Sheela's description. I guess she never felt it.

My play was struck by the fall-out from the media frenzy that surrounded publication of Sheela's tell-all tale. Even though the events had happened decades earlier, the story had significant local impact in Pune and, as a result, nearly all the 500-600 college students who'd responded to our free invitation to see the play failed to show up. Sheela's book had scared them off.

"I don't think my parents would want me to come," said one nervous young undergraduate. Strange. In my days as a student, if my parents didn't want me to do something, it guaranteed that I would. Clearly, the revolutionary fervour that once swept through the campuses of Europe has yet to penetrate the Indian education system.

I have no idea if Sheela's book became a best-seller. But, even if it didn't, it requires an answer. Why? Because, sooner or later, Osho's work is going to gain wider public recognition and when it does I don't want people to get the wrong idea. It's not that I want to put Sheela down, or pretend that in her place I would have done better, but for the history books a few things need to be set straight.

Here's a rough summary of Sheela's version of events:

She and Osho were a team. He needed her as much as she needed him. Together, they were invincible. But then his demands for more and more Rolls-Royces and expensive watches became so excessive that she could not satisfy them while at the same time continuing to finance the commune.

She refused to cooperate and left. Without her leadership and care, the Oregon commune fell apart, dissolving into chaos. Without her guidance, sannyasins misbehaved, refused to work and plundered the commune.

Out of vengefulness, Osho then accused Sheela of a host of crimes, all of which she denied, but for which she made a plea bargain with US Prosecutors and did jail time. In conclusion, she offers a schizophrenic vision: Osho was a wonderful man, a great visionary whom she still loves, but whose character was fatally flawed.

Now, let's set the record straight:

First of all, I can tell you from my own personal

   Anand Subhuti

experience that after Sheela left, in September 1985, the Oregon commune did not fall apart. Nor was it plundered by ungrateful sannyasins, as she claims. On the contrary, as her plane departed, most of us were dancing in the streets with happiness.

I used to like Sheela. But her position as Osho's spokesperson inflated her ego to the point where she actually thought people were as devoted to her as to the mystic himself. Moreover, as political pressure in America mounted, with all kinds of state and federal agencies trying to shut us down, Sheela had become a paranoid control freak and a major pain in the butt. In the end, everyone was happy she'd gone.

Chaos and misbehaviour? Nothing of the kind happened. Not a single mealtime was missed. The commune's department managers, whom Sheela had urged to leave with her, declined her invitation and continued at their posts. Even when Osho was arrested and put in jail by the Reagan Administration, the commune continued to operate smoothly.

It was only when Osho was deported that the commune's new management realised it wouldn't be economically feasible to continue – and I certainly agreed with them. Osho had been the magnet that drew us all to this dreary cattle ranch in Central Oregon, surrounded by gum-chewing rednecks and born-again believers. Without him, the place had zero appeal and zero meaning.

Even then, it didn't fall apart. People left in an orderly fashion, leaving a skeleton crew behind, including myself. We had a great time, living in the Ranch's hotel, enjoying its Tantric circular beds and beautiful outdoor Jacuzzi. Until the last sannyasin left, there was always food on the table. So much for misbehaviour, chaos and plundering.

As for Sheela's alleged crimes, I have seen the affidavits of her former colleagues who gave evidence of her wrongdoing. It's pretty clear she was up to no good – to put it mildly.

However, my focus of interest isn't her crimes. It is the moment she walked out. There was simply no need for it. If she was feeling stressed and exhausted, all she had to do was sit in front of Osho and expose her inability to cope with the demands being made on her. All she had to do was give up her self-image as the superwoman whom Osho needed as much as she needed him.

But she couldn't do it. She couldn't face the possibility that he might say "Okay Sheela, you've done enough. Now I'll find myself a new secretary and you can join the kitchen crew and chop vegetables."

It could have been that simple, just like my shortened version of *Macbeth*. But, no, like Lady Macbeth before her, Sheela couldn't take her hands off the steering wheel and allow events to take their natural course. In short, Sheela was doing fine until she let her appetite for power carry her away. Then everything came unglued. Now she lives in Switzerland, running a couple of old folks' homes and weaving fairy stories to try and excuse her behaviour.

So let's leave her there. I've answered her book and that's enough. Or maybe we should give the final word to my Macbeth:

> *Oh meditators, tell me true,*
> *From your enlightened point of view,*
> *Was my wife a wicked witch?*
> *Or was she just a stupid bitch?*

Anand Subhuti

Chapter Fourteen

Nobody Cares About You

I notice I'm avoiding the delicate subject of Nobody. That's because I'm not sure how to introduce her. Most people know Lewis Carroll's story *Alice Through the Looking Glass*, in which Alice gets involved in a confusing conversation:

"Who did you pass on the road?" the King asked.

"Nobody," said the Messenger.

"Quite right," said the King, "this young lady saw him too. So of course Nobody walks slower than you."

"I do my best," the Messenger said in a sullen tone. "I'm sure Nobody walks much faster than I do!"

"He can't do that," said the King, "or else he'd have been here first."

And so it goes. This is a play on words, invented by the Reverend Charles Dodgson – Lewis Carroll's real name – to amuse a pretty young woman of his acquaintance, Alice Liddell, with whom he was obsessed and infatuated. However, the Rev. Dodgson managed to curb his paedophile passion and instead channelled his lust into a literary masterpiece.

But the Nobody who comes into my play is a very

different character. She introduces the idea of *not to be*, which is crucial if the other characters are to free themselves from their roles and therefore from their miserable fate. *Not to be* is another name for meditation, so I'm trying to introduce this delicate subject into a play without boring the pants off the audience – no mean feat.

We take up the tale where Hamlet is recovering from the traumatic experience of being temporarily dead. He limps across the stage, nursing the wounded leg where Will Shakespeare unkindly stabbed him with a poisoned sword. He sees the skull, sitting beside my chair, and picks it up, as if to deliver the famous soliloquy which, in the original version, begins:

"Alas, poor Yorick, I knew him..."

My interpretation is a little different:

"Alas, poor Yorick! You lost your head over a woman, didn't you? Well, that's not going to happen to me!"

Carelessly, Hamlet tosses the skull over his shoulder. Its sails through the air and lands perilously close to my chair. Fortunately, even if it hit me, it wouldn't do any damage. It's a toy skull made of rubber.

At this moment, Nobody walks on stage. She's wearing blue jeans and a white t-shirt with the word "NOBODY" printed in capital letters across her chest. She has a denim cap, with its peak turned cheekily to one side. Her mood is upbeat and playful, like a small fairy or imp who enjoys the foolishness of mere mortals and once in a while decides to interfere and mess with their heads.

Nobody glances quizzically at Hamlet. "Hi, how's it going?" she inquires.

Hamlet: "Well, to be honest, I could use a few laughs. Who are you? What's your name?"

 Anand Subhuti

Nobody: "Nobody."

Hamlet: "Nobody? C'mon, you must be *somebody*."

Nobody: "Everybody tells me that: 'You *must* be *somebody*.' But *anybody* can be somebody. And everybody *wants* to be somebody. Nobody wants to be *Nobody*. Except me."

Hamlet: "Can you say that again, slowly please?"

Nobody: "Everybody says that, as well. *Nobody* understands."

Hamlet: "But you *are* Nobody, so *you* must understand."

Nobody: "Anybody *could* understand, and I keep thinking one day somebody *will* understand. But believe me, nobody has any idea what Nobody is talking about."

Hamlet: "Well, nobody's perfect."

Nobody: "Thank you, I agree!"

Hamlet: "No, that's not what I meant!"

Nobody: "No worries. Nobody cares."

What Nobody is saying here, is not just a play on words. She's touching on a subject close to our hearts: the desire in all of us to be somebody. Everybody wants to be special, which, when you think about it, immediately makes our common desire un-special, precisely because everybody has it.

If you find this confusing, let me allow Osho to say it his own words: "The desire to be extraordinary is a very ordinary desire. Everybody has it. To be ordinary is really extraordinary."

To which, you may sensibly inquire: "Okay, but what's the pay-off in being ordinary? What's in it for me?" Patience. All will be revealed at the appropriate time.

Hamlet: "Okay, Mister Nobody, where are you from?"

Nobody: "I'm from the Land of Not To Be."

Hamlet (sarcastically): "I should have guessed."

Nobody: "Not to be, you see, is the only way to be,

Though you may disagree, just listen carefully:

The more you think you've got, the more you have to drop.

But, the more you find you're not, the more you've really got."

Hamlet: "That's nonsense, don't you see? Or would nobody agree?"

Nobody: "Nonsense it may be, but would you agree, to check it out with me?"

Hamlet: "Well, okay... maybe."

Nobody: "Watch closely... you will see."

At this point, Queen Elizabeth and her two attendants arrive on stage. In their company, we are transported to her Royal Court, where the daily business of the realm is being conducted. One of the attendants unrolls a scroll containing supplications to the Crown. My aim here is to reinforce the queen's image as a cold-hearted bitch, in urgent need of transformation.

By the way, I must emphasize that the queen's gold dress looked great, a triumph for Ritu's tailoring, and as for the floppy ruff... well, my dear friend carried it off as best she could. How the original queen's dressmakers managed it, I have no idea. Either it was, as I have already speculated, whalebone, or they used enough starch to stiffen the River Thames.

The day's Royal business continues:

First Attendant: "Your Majesty, the people of London have no bread to eat."

Elizabeth: "Let them eat cake."

A line borrowed, of course, from Marie Antoinette, who, by

   Anand Subhuti

the way, never said it but got her head chopped anyway.

First Attendant: "Your Majesty, the people of York say your taxes are too high."

Elizabeth: "Let them work harder."

First Attendant, with a big toady grin on his face: "Your Majesty, the people of Lancaster wish you a happy birthday."

Elizabeth allows a small, contemptuous smile to lighten up her grim features: "Indeed? How touching. Let them make a statue of me, in gratitude."

Today's business is concluded and the Royal trio freeze, standing motionless on the stage.

Nobody: "Tell me, who is she?"

Hamlet: "Of course, 'tis Her Majesty."

To Hamlet's amazement, Nobody walks over to the trio and reaches up, as if to take away Queen Elizabeth's crown.

Nobody: "And if I remove her attire?"

Hamlet is alarmed at the prospect of such a foolhardy act: "Oh, I wouldn't do that, sire!"

Not in the least worried, Nobody gently lifts the crown from Queen Elizabeth's head. The Queen, otherwise motionless, gasps as she feels the crown being taken away. Nobody gives the crown to one of the Queen's attendants and turns once more to address Hamlet.

Nobody: "Who is this woman now, before whom you love to bow?"

Hamlet: "Well, no matter what it seems, she will still say she's the queen."

Nobody: "Without a crown with golden teeth?"

Hamlet: "Why certainly, 'tis her belief."

Nobody: "This belief, she wears it like a mask. So this

gives me another task."

Again, she approaches Queen Elizabeth and gently removes the golden mask from her face, leaving her looking vulnerable and astonished. And again, the Queen gasps as if being robbed of her status and power.

Hamlet can't quite believe what he's seeing and in an aside to the audience, whispers: "This Nobody is quite insane,

She'll cut his head and eat his brains!"
Nobody: "Your queen is stripped of power and glory
Who is she now in your Tudor story?"
Hamlet: "Why, looking simple, sad and sorry
This woman is just... ordinary."

Exactly. That's the very point Nobody wishes to emphasize. While the denuded Queen looks out across the audience, dazed and confused, asking "Who am I?" Nobody seizes this opportunity to coach Hamlet on how transformation works.

Nobody: Hamlet, you have hit upon the truth
And now the Queen will give you living proof
Now anything can happen, you will see
How 'not to be' makes everybody free...

This is where things get surreal. Modern pop music with a hip-hop flavour starts to play and Nobody pulls Hamlet to one side as Mrs Shakespeare and Ophelia come onstage in tight, black, sexy leotards and perform a passable imitation of Beyonce's 'All The Single Ladies' dance routine. It's cool, it's slick, it's unmistakeably 21st century and therefore has nothing to do with Elzabethan England. Only Nobody could pull off a time-warp stunt like this.

The Queen remains under some kind of hypnotic spell, cast upon her by Nobody, and she is enchanted by these two women, watching their moves closely. She has forgotten all about her royal dignity and prudery. When the music suddenly stops, Elizabeth has only one thing in mind.

Elizabeth: What is this dancing that you do?

Can I learn to dance with you?

Mrs Shakespeare: Dear Madam, come and dance with us.

Ophelia: We'll show you how to shake your ass.

The music starts again and the Queen makes a hilarious sight, trying to dance like Beyonce in her long royal robes. Here, the medium is the message. I'm not sure if Canadian philosopher Marshall McLuhan meant it this way, when he coined the famous expression back in the 60s, but what we're seeing is a visual illustration of what happens when we drop our attachment to a certain public image and let our energy freely express itself.

However, the good times don't last long. After a few minutes, the music stops once more and simultaneously the spell begins to wear off. The Queen is emerging from her trance and returning to her old self. Mrs Shakespeare and Ophelia look apprehensive.

Ophelia: Uh-oh, I think we're in trouble.

Mrs Shakespeare: Get ready to run.

Predictably, the Queen is outraged by the sight of these two skimpily clad female forms. Her next move is equally predictable:

"What is happening in my court? These women are naked! Off with their heads! Off with their heads!"

Mrs Shakespeare and Ophelia run off, pursued by the Queen and her attendants. Nobody, slightly disappointed by this turn of events, watches her go, then shrugs his shoulders.

Nobody: "Of course, it doesn't always work.

That Elizabeth is such a stupid jerk!"
He turns to Hamlet:
"Now, Hamlet, think what I have said,
Take off *your* mask and lose *your* head!"
Hamlet is genuinely confused: "I have no mask! It's not on me."
Nobody laughs: "Oh yes, you have. You just can't see!"
Hamlet gets irritated: "You've gone quite mad, I'll say good day!
And this Nobody can go his way."
He starts to walk away, but Nobody catches him gently by the arm to prevent him. This is the moment of truth. If Hamlet can understand that he's wearing a false mask of personality, just like the queen, he can achieve a breakthrough. But, since I don't want this play to become preachy, it needs to happen playfully.
Nobody: "Wait, spare a moment, let me ask,
This noble fellow with no mask,
This gloomy guy so filled with sadness
Who thinks that I am touched by madness.
Can you smile and sing and dance
If I give you half a chance?"
Hamlet: "Of course I can, if I so choose.
I've really nothing left to lose."
Nobody: "Then why be miserable and glum
When you can dance under the sun?"
Hamlet: "It isn't me who feels this way..."
He points at Will, sitting in his chair, scribbling away.
"...it's this bloody Bard who writes this play!"
Nobody seizes the opportunity presented by Hamlet's remark.
Nobody: "Come then, let's show this anti-fun guy

　　　　Anand Subhuti

How they move it down in Mumbai!"

Cue for a Bollywood song and dance routine. The part of Nobody is, as I've said before, played by a young Indian woman. She practices Cranio-Sacral therapy but in her heart she's a dancer and a showgirl – she's been in all my musicals. So it's completely natural for her to boogie onstage, doing those classic Bollywood moves that we've all seen in Hindi movies.

Hamlet watches her and does his best to follow, but can't get the hang of it. Eventually, he gives up.

Hamlet: "Stop! Stop! Enough! It's plain to see,

This Bollywood is not for me."

Nobody is disappointed. She folds her arms and looks at Hamlet in disgust.

"You're giving up because you're foreign?

Oh Hamlet, this is really boring!"

But she's in for a surprise.

Hamlet: "But I *can* dance, please have no fear,

He takes out a pair of sunglasses, puts then on and gives the audience a frighteningly wide smile.

"Hi! My name's Psy... I'm from Korea!

Dressing classy, dancing cheesy

Gangnam Style is really easy!"

If there's one moment in the play which is really surprising and has the audience gasping in delight, it's this sudden transition from Hamlet to Psy. Born of Korean parents, all this actor has to do is put on a pair of sunglasses and start making those famous moves we've all seen on YouTube's record-breaking *Gangnam Style* video. Two billion people can't be wrong. The whole audience cracks up.

Hamlet leaps across the stage and drags me into the act, as well as Mrs Shakespeare and Ophelia, so when the music takes off we suddenly go, all together, into Psy's cowboy dance routine. Pretty soon, I'm standing at the front of the stage with my legs apart, doing hip thrusts, while Hamlet is lying on the floor, poking his head through – another classic scene from the video. The song ends with enthusiastic applause from the audience.

Will Shakespeare staggers to the front of the stage, shakes his head, and exclaims, "My god, what in the name of Her Majesty is happening to my play? I will be thrown into the Tower of London and left to rot forever!"

An aside from the author: At this point in the play I seriously considered having the Bard stand on his head, in the classic yoga position of *sirsana*. It would be a perfect metaphor for what is happening to him. But I gave up the idea for two reasons: first, it would take too long and second, at the age of 67, I can't guarantee I'd manage it.

Instead, Will returns to his seat and continues writing. Meanwhile, Hamlet is beginning to realise that Nobody's peculiar but intriguing way of looking at life might be just the thing he needs to escape his gloomy destiny. He wants to know more.

Hamlet: "Okay Mr. Nobody, I'm beginning to see things differently. But there's one thing I don't understand. What would I gain from becoming a *Not To Be*?"

Nobody: "Well, let's see... you wouldn't be the Prince of Denmark any more... so you wouldn't be obsessed with trying to avenge your father's death... so you wouldn't spend all your time thinking "to be or not to be"... *and* you wouldn't tell your beautiful girlfriend to get lost."

Hamlet: "Really?"

Nobody: "Really."

Hamlet: "How do I do it?"

 Anand Subhuti

Nobody: "Ah, that can be a *little* challenging. Come with me."

Here, we are approaching the crucial moment in the play when I try to show how people can escape from their own psychological limitations through meditation. Not an easy task, let me tell you, especially with the twin threats of sermonising and proselytising hanging over my head.

But Hamlet is ready to make the change and so, it turns out, is Ophelia. As Hamlet leaves with Nobody, she comes on stage with Mrs Shakespeare.

Ophelia: "Oh Mrs. Shakespeare, it was wonderful being Lady Raga. But I don't want to imitate anybody else. I want to be me."

Mrs Shakespeare: "Really?"

Ophelia: "Really."

Mrs Shakespeare: "Really... really?"

Ophelia: "Yes really. I just want to be myself."

Mrs Shakespeare: "Well, that can be a *little* challenging. Come with me."

The stage is set for a visual presentation of spiritual transformation. Let's hope we don't fall flat on our faces.

Chapter Fifteen

Good Thoughts, Bad Thoughts

Queen Elizabeth sweeps imperiously onto the stage and spies the object of her wrath – the luckless Bard. Instinctively, she knows that something is amiss. With long experience from her tenuous grip on a shaky English throne, she senses the rebellious atmosphere brewing here among the players. She intends to stomp on it without further ado.

"Master Shakespeare, we are not pleased with the way this play is progressing," she informs him.

Will sinks to one knee and bows his head. He's in an impossible situation, stretched to breaking point between Her Majesty's demand for tragedy and his wife's determination to do everything in her power to sabotage it.

"A thousand apologies Your Majesty," he stutters.

"We have not yet seen enough suffering and death to call it a tragedy."

Will's cunning mind searches for an escape route. Smiling in a show of pathetic submissiveness to the Royal Presence, he stalls for time.

"Fear not, Your Majesty..."

Fear not? He's the one filled with fear, quaking in his boots under the queen's fierce stare. Like a drowning man clutching at straws, he offers a feeble explanation:

"I'm... er... I'm planning a surprise. The play will seem to be heading in the direction of happiness, but, at the very end, I shall kill them all, I swear it!"

Her Majesty is mollified, up to a point, but there's a sting in her tail.

"Very well. See that it is done..." her tone becomes more menacing... "or I promise you, thine head shall be impaled on a stake before the Tower of London!"

Just what a desperate playwright needs to hear.

"Oh no! I mean... oh yes, Your Majesty." He bows low with grovelling humility as the Queen strides away, then returns to his chair to write the ending she commands.

Meanwhile, the rebellion continues. Two chairs are brought to the middle of the stage and placed facing the audience. Nobody brings Hamlet and indicates he should sit on one chair. Mrs Shakespeare brings Ophelia and asks her to sit in the other. Then Nobody and Mrs Shakespeare explain the basic guidelines for this exercise, in which they will help Hamlet and Ophelia free themselves from their identities.

"*Not To Be* requires an empty mind," says Nobody.

"A clear and quiet head," confirms Mrs Shakespeare.

Pointing to herself and to the Bard's wife, Nobody continues, "We will represent your thoughts."

"When a thought enters your head, we will speak it for you," adds Mrs Shakespeare.

"In this way, you will become aware of your own thoughts," continues Nobody.

"And most important, you will become aware of the silence *behind* your thoughts," instructs Will's wife.

Nobody concludes, "In that silence you will discover the *Land of Not To Be*."

Okay, so let me review the build-up so far, just to prevent any misunderstanding. Onstage it's pretty clear, but in print it might seem a little confusing.

Ophelia is desperate to break out of her role as the fated, rejected lover of Hamlet. She tasted liberation as Lady Raga and now wants more. Hamlet is less certain what he wants, but after a wild dance routine as Psy in *Gangnam Style*, he realizes he's missing out on life.

From a sannyasin perspective, they're both in the situation of a spiritual seeker who realizes he is trapped in his personality and wants out. Perhaps I should add, here, that relatively few people ever come to this point. Most people are more or less satisfied with who they are – or at least pretend to be.

Osho's idea about meditation? You can't experience yourself as pure consciousness while you're identified with your personality. Why? Because your personality is your outer-most layer, while consciousness is your innermost centre. If you're glued to the outside edge of a circle, you can't go in to the middle.

Let's take a look, for a moment, at the common British expression "Who the hell do you think you are?" We use it to address someone who is being arrogant. But, in reality, this saying applies to all of us. Thinking creates who we are. It's our ideas about ourselves that create personality and, of course, we've been collecting these ideas ever since we were born, so there's going to be lots of them.

So, how do we free ourselves from all this? According

     Anand Subhuti

to Osho, we do it by learning to watch our own thoughts. He often uses the metaphor of a 'watcher on the hill' in which we observe thoughts passing through the mind, like someone sitting on a hillside, watching cars passing on a highway below.

As soon as we become aware of a thought, it loses its grip on us. For example, Ophelia feels hurt that Hamlet has dumped her. But if she becomes *aware* she is hurt, a distance opens up between herself and her emotion. Through this distance, she may come to realise that she is not the emotion. She will still feel the pain, but it won't totally consume her.

I'm not saying this is easy. Not at all. Most probably, when you've just been dumped by your boyfriend, you want to kill him, or jump off a cliff, or post nasty remarks on *Facebook* about his new girlfriend. The last thing you want to do is sit down, close your eyes, meditate and realise that you're not your emotions.

This is hard work. It's not like instant coffee. Most people don't have the time for it, nor the dedication needed to patiently explore their inner world. But, like it or not, that's the name of the game played by Osho's sannyasins and that's what I'm trying to convey in this scene.

One more thing: over time, when you meditate, a kind of flexibility is gained. You're not so controlled by your personality. You become more authentic, more real, because your way of thinking arises from a deeper source within you. That's the payoff.

"Close your eyes. Let us begin," says Mrs Shakespeare. She and Nobody then crouch down behind the chairs on which Hamlet and Ophelia are sitting. Mrs Shakespeare hides behind Ophelia, Nobody is behind Hamlet. When a thought enters Hamlet's head, Nobody will jump up and speak it aloud. The same goes for Mrs Shakespeare and Ophelia.

Nobody goes first. She stands up, cups her ear to listen to what's going on inside Hamlet's head and declares: "This is easy... oh no, that's a thought!" His thought vanishes and she ducks down.

Mrs Shakespeare stands up, listens to the chatter inside Ophelia's head and announces: "I just want to be myself." Puzzled, Mrs Shakespeare remains standing, turns to look at Nobody and asks: "Is this a thought?"

Nobody stands up, surprised at the question: "Of course it is!"

"But it's such a nice thought," objects Mrs Shakespeare, not ready to let it go.

Nobody shakes her head impatiently: "Nice thoughts... nasty thoughts... they all have to go!"

Mrs Shakespeare shrugs. "Oh well... bye bye nice thought!" she says and they both duck down behind the chairs.

Now here's a thought: many people who meditate make a distinction between good thoughts and bad thoughts. Indeed, the whole American philosophy of 'positive thinking' is based on the idea that spirituality can be cultivated by disposing of negative thoughts and emphasising positive ones.

How does that old show tune go?

> *You Gotta Akk-Sent-Chew-Ate the Positive,*
> *Eee-Limmm-In-Ate the Negative*
> *That's what gets results!*

Anand Subhuti

To Osho, this is childish. Meditation has nothing to do with good and bad. It's a method of dis-identifying with the mind *in its totality*, regardless of content. So meditators are neither moral nor immoral people. They go beyond the duality.

Nobody rises from behind Hamlet's chair, picking up a thought: "I'm hungry!" She declares, rubbing her stomach, then ducks down.

Mrs Shakespeare rises, speaks for Ophelia and announces: "I'm thirsty!"

Thoughts follow in rapid succession:

Nobody: "I'm restless."

Mrs Shakespeare: "I'm sad."

Nobody: "To be or not to be?... oh, not again!"

Then Ophelia sinks a little deeper, into her heart, and Mrs Shakespeare echoes a poignant thought arising from this sweet young woman's breast: "I wonder if Hamlet still loves me?"

Hamlet's mind, on the other hand, is straying in a slightly different direction, which Nobody picks up.

Nobody: "I wonder what Ophelia looks like in the shower?" She interrupts the action by looking at Mrs Shakespeare and exclaiming "Now there's an interesting thought!"

Mrs Shakespeare is uncomfortable with this unexpected turn of events. Standing up, she looks indignantly at Nobody and protests, "Hey, keep your mind on your job, *Mister Not To Be!*"

Nobody doesn't mind the rebuke. She's more interested in what's going on inside Hamlet's head.

"Well, it's the first time he's actually expressed interest in her," she explains.

Mrs Shakespeare leaves her post and comes to stand behind Hamlet. Giving the audience her very best, deeply ironic smile, she places her two hands gently on Hamlet's head and declares "Isn't the male mind wonderful? If it's not drowning women in lakes, it's gazing at them under the shower."

This produces a big laugh from the audience, especially from the women. But then Nobody raises a hand to interrupt her.

"Wait... Listen! Listen!"

"What do you hear?" asks Mrs Shakespeare.

With a big smile, as if announcing the winner of the National Lottery, Nobody gestures towards the sitting couple and says, "Nothing!"

Mrs Shakespeare was so caught up in her feminist view of male psychology that she forgot, temporarily, the purpose of the exercise. Now she realises just how successful it's been. Joining Nobody in her delight, she looks at Hamlet and Ophelia, who are both still sitting with eyes closed, and exclaims in triumph to the audience, "Oh my god, they've done it. They've stopped thinking!"

Nobody and Mrs Shakespeare turn towards each other, each raising a finger to her lips and softly hissing: "Sssshhhhh!" Then, joining the lovers in this unexpected moment of deep meditation, they both close their eyes and stand in silence behind Hamlet and Ophelia.

There is the long dramatic pause. Meditation has dawned and all four minds are quiet. The gateway to the Beyond has opened.

I'm not sure if this has ever been done onstage before, although variations have manifested in several movies, most notably in the 1954 Japanese epic, *The Seven Samurai*,

     Anand Subhuti

and more recently in *The Last Samurai*, where Tom Cruise, as US Army Captain Nathan Algren, is seen training as a samurai in a remote mountain village. Tom keeps getting beaten in mock fights until a friendly warrior tells him he has 'too many minds' and needs a quick dose of 'no mind' if he is to be victorious.

Stretching his modest acting abilities to the maximum, Tom closes his eyes for a second and then, presumably with a blank space between his ears, charges at his foe. Presto! His combat skills acquire an extra edge and he earns an honourable draw in the contest.

Oh Tom, if only it was that easy...

As any experienced meditator knows, it's difficult to remain in the space of no-mind for more than a few seconds. Sooner or later, a thought is going to arise that will grab your attention and carry you off.

In my play, it's Mrs Shakespeare who cracks first. Opening her eyes and looking slightly vacant, as if trying to remember something important, she gently bites on one of her fingers and ponders, "I wonder if I left my cooking pot on the stove?"

Mind is like that. It keeps throwing thoughts at you until eventually one catches your interest and you start chewing on it.

Nobody rolls her eyes in frustration. "Oy vey! Now *you're* thinking!" she protests.

But Mrs Shakespeare refuses to be embarrassed so easily and quickly retorts, "Well, now *you're* thinking about me thinking."

This kind of spiritual one-upmanship can continue indefinitely, with characters accusing each other of thinking about them thinking about them thinking...

But Nobody has noticed Ophelia is slowly opening her eyes. He raises a hand to stop their little tiff.

"Wait! She's going to say something," she informs Mr Shakespeare, pointing towards Ophelia.

What words of wisdom will be uttered by this young vision of loveliness, now that she been to no-mind and back? Will she reject Hamlet? Will she still be hooked? What does the future hold for these sweet young people?

We will know soon enough. But first, a few words about the state of meditation from which she is emerging. Quantum physics would probably consider it to be similar to the Zero Point Field Theory, which asserts that even when there are no particles present in a given field, some kind of wave-like energy still persists.

In other words, even when there is nothing, there is something. Likewise with consciousness: even when there are no thoughts, there is something we might describe as... *the great nothing.*

 Anand Subhuti

Chapter Sixteen

The Great Nothing

*H*ere's the skinny, the bottom line, the low-down on how we experience our inner world: *Nothing happens.*

On the outside, everything is continuously changing. Even mountains are changing, eroding slowly over time; even suns and galaxies are born, grow old and die. But on the inside, nothing ever happens.

Or, as writer Ernest Hemingway might say, after introducing the Spanish word for 'nothing' into the American language... 'Nada.'

Hemingway took it negatively and felt that the universe is indifferent to us. He used the idea of *nada* to illustrate man's struggle in a life where God is absent and existence is at best neutral and at worst downright hostile towards human beings.

In protest, he spoofed the Lord's Prayer thus: 'Our nada who art in nada, nada be thy name, thy kingdom nada...' It was a tribute to the author's nihilistic and accidental view of the universe.

John-Paul Sartre and the Existentialists of the 1950s struggled with the idea of nothingness. On the one hand, it was attractive because it freed man's consciousness from the grip of divine will and pre-determination. But, at the same time, it made everything meaningless. Unlike Hemingway, however, Sartre declined to blow his brains out as an existential solution to this philosophical problem.

Hemmingway and Sartre are not exceptions. Generally speaking, nothingness has been given a bad rap in Western culture. Why? Because people are afraid of it. It implies an absence of meaning, morality and value in our lives... scary stuff.

The greatest children's story ever written – ignoring Harry Potter and leaving aside my personal favourites, Rupert Bear and Winnie the Pooh – is the epic German fantasy novel by Michael Ende called *The Neverending Story*.

The tale takes place in a fabulous world called Fantastica, which is being destroyed by a mysterious force. This terrible, unstoppable force eats up all the beautiful, strange and wonderful characters of Fantastica, who can only be rescued by a human child participating in the story.

And what, one may ask, is the name Michael Ende gives to this dark force? *The Nothing*. This provides us with an intriguing insight into the writer's mind. It seems that nothingness is regarded by Ende as the ultimate threat, the destructive opposite of creative fantasy and imagination.

In the tale itself, The Nothing is explained as the effect of all the lies humans tell in their greed for power, but I happen to know Ende really was afraid of nothingness. Late in life, he told a friend of mine – just back from India – that he felt Europeans should stick to Western methods of meditation and not experiment with Eastern techniques.

Carl Gustav Jung, one of the founders of modern

     Anand Subhuti

psychology, said more or less the same thing after his own trip to India in 1937, where he studied Hinduism and became greatly interested in Ramana Maharshi, an enlightened mystic who, at the time, was living on Mount Arunachala in South India.

Jung described Ramana as 'something quite phenomenal' and a 'true son of the Indian earth' who had 'struggled earnestly all his life to extinguish his ego'. But Jung shied away from meeting the man, fearing his own understanding of the human psyche would be shaken if he encountered Ramana personally. He also advised Westerners against dabbling in yoga and other Eastern methods of meditation.

What was the fear? The basic difference between East and West is that the Western approach to spirituality is a form of contemplation, or prayer, and thus remains within the realm of intellectual thought. Western philosophy does the same. Renee Descartes, the 17th century Frenchman who is regarded as 'the father of modern philosophy', summed it up in his famous declaration "I think therefore I am."

About 300 years later, my philosophy professors at Bristol arrogantly informed me they had improved on Decartes. All that can really be said, they argued, is: "There is a thought." You cannot rationally infer "I am" from the thinking process.

However, if Gautam Buddha had been passing through Bristol at the time, he might have asked them "How do you know? How do you know there is a thought? There must be a deeper sense of 'amness' that is aware of the thought, otherwise you wouldn't be able to say even this much."

Siddhartha is right. Consciousness precedes cognition.

Western philosophy stops here, because it depends on thought for its existence. No thought, no philosophy. Of course, some academic who enjoys playing mind games can easily write a book titled *The Philosophy of No Thinking* (I can even be accused of doing this myself), but make no mistake, the author of such a book is only thinking about not thinking. He isn't *not thinking*. If he's not thinking, he's not a philospher. He's a meditator.

Eastern meditation embraces no thought, or nothingness, and that's what Descartes didn't get, and both Jung and Ende didn't want to know. I'm sure the Bard would have sided with Jung, Ende and Descartes because none of them understood that, in reality, all things – from children's stories to the human mind to the universe itself – arise from the creative womb of no-thing, or nothingness. They couldn't fathom the paradox that you can't have *something* without *nothing*. They didn't realize the two go together. Modern physics is coming closer to this understanding, but it'll take a while.

Eckhart Tolle, a spiritual teacher who seems to know what he's talking about, encourages people to explore the gaps between their thoughts. That's how you plug into what Tolle calls 'space consciousness' – a fancy name for nothingness.

To most of us, such practices seem unappealing because all you find is... well... nothing. But if you go deeper you may be fortunate enough to experience another awesome paradox:

"This nothingness is not negative," explained Osho, while discussing the Big Zero. "Just a little more acquaintance with it and you will be surprised, you start feeling an immense fulfilment and overflowing energy.

                    Anand Subhuti

This nothingness is the beginning of fullness and wholeness."

Shall I tell you the truth? *Tat Tvam Asi... that art thou.* The ancient seers of the Vedas knew their stuff when they declared that *you are it.* When everything you think you are has disappeared, only space consciousness remains... and hey, guess what? That's you.

So, to Ernest Hemingway, Jean Paul Sartre, Michael Ende and Carl Jung, I need to say: bite the bullet, guys, and face it. Like it or not, you are *The Nothing.*

Nothing and non-doing go hand in hand. It's only when you're doing nothing, *not even thinking about doing nothing,* that space consciousness manifests itself and the sound of one hand clapping deafens your inner eardrums.

Even when you sit down to 'do' meditation, you're off-base, which poses a tricky problem for mystics like Osho who want to encourage others to experience the inner world. Every meditation technique, however subtle, is a kind of effort, a kind of doing, so, how to give people a taste of no-mind?

Osho hit on the idea of using opposite extremes. He encouraged people to be vigorously active in the first half of a meditation, then relax and let go of all effort in the second half. The principle was simple: intense activity creates the opportunity for its polar opposite, non-doing, to arise naturally.

"Doing cannot lead to being..." I remember some New Age guru uttering this apparently wise statement. But it's not the whole truth, because if you exhaust yourself through doing, you have a much better chance of relaxing into being. However, I need to point out that 'doing' is a modern disease and that's why active meditations are necessary. We are so busy, so mentally stressed, so physically tense, that we need to 'overdo' and release all this pent-up pressure before we can relax.

It wasn't always so, especially in India. This place got its reputation for being a country full of bone lazy people because, for centuries and centuries, non-doing and meditation were embraced and even respected as a way of life.

This reminds me of a story, told by Osho and others, concerning the first railroad track ever to be laid in India, sometime towards the end of the 19th century. A gang of local labourers was working hard, laying track, under the supervision of a British engineer.

Every day, a young Indian man, dressed only in a simple *lunghi* or sarong, would come and sit under a nearby tree and watch the work as it progressed.

The engineer noticed the young man's regular appearance at his viewing spot and eventually became curious. One day, he walked over to the tree and asked the young man, "What are you doing here?"

"Nothing," he replied.

The engineer snorted his disapproval. "You should come and work for me," he advised.

"How would that benefit me?" the young man enquired.

"Well, if you work hard, you will soon be able to earn a considerable sum of money," the engineer explained.

"And what would I do with this money?" asked the young man.

"When you have saved enough money, you will be able to relax and enjoy life," said the engineer.

The young man laughed and shook his head, saying

"But I'm relaxed and enjoying now!"

I don't know if this incident really happened, but it nicely enshrines the old India and its lifestyle, contrasted with modern Western values. Of course, it's all changing now. You walk along a street in Bangalore today and you think you're in New York City – the hustle is infectious and you can sense the urgent, hungry feeling that money is just waiting to be made in India's software capital. And remember, time is money!

That's not how it used to be. The lingering atmosphere of a vanishing subcontinent awash with idleness was still present when I landed at Mumbai airport in 1976. Everything was slower, less important. Time stretched forever, forwards and backwards both.

You wish to be rich? Hey Ram! If god so wills, one day it may happen. If not in this life, maybe in the next...

The taxi that conveyed me from the airport to the train station was old and rusty. Its AC wasn't working. When we turned off the highway, traffic was mostly bullock carts, bicycles and lots and lots of people walking on foot. Nobody seemed to be in a hurry.

When I got to the station, families were eating and sleeping on the ground in the entrance hall, their packages spread out around them, as if their trains were days away from departure. When I got to the counter, the ticket seller had gone for chai, but anyway it wasn't a problem because my train was an hour late. And, more important than any of these separate incidents: *none of it seemed to matter.*

Getting something done could be terribly frustrating, but only until you realized it didn't need doing in the first place. For example, trying to find an electrician to fix a wall socket in my rented Pune apartment drove me nuts, until I gave up trying to fix it. Later, when it was finally fixed, it looked worse than before.

Indians hate to be reminded of those days, when any kind of service was simply lousy. That's why Prince Philip, England's favourite racist, caused such a stink in 1999 when he looked at a scrambled mass of wires in a fuse box, while touring some factory, and commented, "It looks as though it was put in by an Indian."

Hey Ram! I never thought I'd agree with old Phil about anything, but we are both nostalgic for a bygone era of sub-continental ineptitude and indolence. It's far from politically correct, I agree, but it contains a great secret, now in danger of being lost forever.

Oh, the peace that comes with non-doing! I remember one warm and sunny morning, sitting for hours on a tree stump in a run-down park in Pune called 'Empress Gardens' named after the late, great Queen Victoria.

At first I was restless, waiting for a friend who hadn't showed up, but slowly, slowly, the atmosphere of non-doing got to me. Little by little, I understood the real reason why I'd come to Empress Gardens. Not to meet anyone. Not to do anything. Not to think about anything. No, I'd come to be seduced by an ancient, invisible, underlying atmosphere of nothingness that was permeating the very air I was breathing.

I stopped looking at my watch. I stopped fidgeting and somehow, for a while, I even stopped thinking.

Pretty soon, I was listening in awe to the silence, feeling the stillness in my bones, gratefully sensing the relief and relaxation in my heart. Nothing was happening, inside or out. No motors running, no car horns blaring, no

 Anand Subhuti

radios playing, no ring tones chiming, no machine tools hammering". Nothing. Even the occasional birdsong only served to deepen the silence in which each sweet note arose and disappeared.

Here, I understood, was the doorway to a different world in which nobody needed to do anything. Here, time stopped. Here, the most to which one might aspire, after several hours of inactivity, would be to rise slowly to one's feet and stroll to a local street stall in search of a delicious, sugar-saturated cup of chai.

Here, and only here, in this precious space, might one bow down in awe to those compassionate mystics who, not content to remain in their blissful silence, tried to make the deaf hear, the blind see, the sleeping humanity awaken... no task for the faint-hearted.

In any case, on that April morning in Empress Gardens, it was way too hot to do anything. When you pass through the hot season in India, you understand how a culture of non-doing is born.

Perhaps it's just as well that meditation didn't become popular in the United States back in the 50s, when the Un-American Activities Committee of Congress was busy rooting out communists and other social deviants. Meditation is neither communist nor anti-communist, but it is, essentially, un-American.

Why? Because Americans are great doers. All their cultural icons, from Superman to Batman, from Dirty Harry to John McClane, are action heroes. The whole nation is hooked on hyperactivity... doing something, getting somewhere, *making it happen.*

Let us reflect on John F. Kennedy's famous utterance: "My fellow Americans, ask not what your country can do for you. Ask what you can do for your country." Either way, it's the 'doing' that's important, right Jack?

JFK certainly practiced what he preached. He was a hyperactive president, always on the go. When he wasn't busy 'doing' government business, he was busy 'doing' White House intern Mimi Alford and many other women who willingly lined up and lay down for 'Jack the Zipper'.

Now, for a moment, stop and think of all the labour saving devices that have been invented in the United States since the 1950s. You'd expect, by now, that everyone would be on permanent holiday – nobody would need to do anything. But no. Paradoxically, introducing faster and more efficient technology has made us faster, too, as if we must run to keep up with it, becoming ever more busy and stressed.

And none of it has helped us become richer. If you believe the statistics, a middle income couple who are both working today generate no greater wealth, in real terms, than in those unliberated days when the wife kept house and the guy earned the bread. *Hey Ram!* That's progress.

Meditation is the exact opposite of this all-American attitude. It is the art of enjoying inactivity, of relaxing into *that which is* – unhooked from the idealism of *becoming*. It is feeling so at ease with life that you naturally and effortlessly sink deeper and deeper into yourself, coming closer and closer to the core... and there, and there alone, you find the fulfilment you have been seeking in a thousand different ways elsewhere.

In short, it is a revolution, a 180-degree turn. And it is a revolution whose time has come.

Chai, anyone?

 Anand Subhuti

Chapter Seventeen

Happy Ever After

This is the moment. Now is the hour. Hamlet and Ophelia are free. They have experienced the silence behind their thoughts. They have entered the land of *Not To Be.* They have dived into the inner ocean and returned.

Practically speaking, this is a bit of a stretch. To have such deep experiences, spiritual seekers sometimes need to meditate for as long as 30 years, maybe even several lifetimes. Theatrically speaking, however, we need to do the job in a few minutes. After all, you can't stop the show and tell the audience: "Come back in a couple of decades and we'll show you what happens next."

Nobody and Mrs Shakespeare stand waiting behind the lovers. What will happen now? What will be their response, now that they understand they are no longer confined within the limitations of their former attitudes?

Slowly, Ophelia opens her eyes and turns her lovely head towards the man she loves.

"Hamlet," she says softly, "You still love me, don't you?"

Hamlet slowly opens his eyes, now fresh with innocence, and turns to look at Ophelia.

He smiles. "Yes, I do," he replies gently.

Ophelia's heart bursts with joy and her face becomes radiant as the secret hope she has been nursing for so long comes true at last. As a theatrical aside, I must add that this scene is greatly assisted by the fact that Ophelia and Hamlet are lovers in real life, so Ophelia has no trouble at all showing her love for this man. It overflows like a fountain from her heart.

"I knew it!" she cries, in relief and happiness.

The first notes of a beautiful song begin to play and Hamlet rises from his seat, turns towards Ophelia, bows slightly and enquires, "Shall we dance?"

"I'd love to," she replies.

The song to which they dance is original. I wrote the lyrics and a friend added the music. It's titled *A Country Far Away* and the opening lines go like this:

> *There is a country far away,*
> *There is a land, far away and lost.*
> *There is a healing, there is a feeling,*
> *There is a country, a country of the heart...*

Who says I'm not an incurable romantic? I recorded the song last year with a sannyasin woman from Taiwan with a fabulous voice and many other showbiz talents. She's the only person I've ever seen tap-dancing in the Pune ashram and she puts Fred Astaire to shame.

The way Hamlet and Ophelia dance is formal, Elizabethan-style. There's lots of ritualistic parting and coming together, with little body contact. Nevertheless, it's an opportunity for them to show the deep affection that flows between them, now all obstacles have been removed. It's a metaphor for making love.

Touched by this romantic scene, Mrs Shakespeare skips lightly across the stage, grabs her husband by the hand and invites him to dance. He tries to refuse, not wishing to indulge in such nonsense, but he's no match for her persuasiveness. Gently, she brings Will to his feet and soon they are dancing together, adding to the harmonious atmosphere.

By the way, I do need to add a word of caution here, lest those romantics among you start thinking that meditation is a sure-fire recipe for solving relationship problems and guaranteeing blissful reunions.

Not exactly. You see, it all depends on what kind of authentic feeling you discover inside yourself, beneath the superficial layers. For example, Ophelia may have opened her eyes, looked at Hamlet and said, "I understand now that you're not the man for me. Goodbye and thank you."

You never know. At this stage in the play, however, it looks like Hamlet and Ophelia are heading towards a happy ending. So let's hit the theatrical pause button for a moment and take a deeper look at the mystery called 'love'.

To be blessed by the love of a woman and to make her feel loved in return is one of the sweetest experiences available to us human beings. It's a kind of magic that descends when two people open their hearts, allowing themselves to merge and complete each other.

Life acquires new meaning, new significance, thanks to this person holding your hand, gazing in your eyes, lying next to you at night. You can't get enough of each other and trivial non-essentials like eating food, going to work, paying bills and staying in touch with the rest of humanity just fade into the background.

The experience of love is real – I want to make this clear. But, at the same time, biology and society are boosting the experience to dangerous heights, rather like a bull run on the stock market that gets out of control and everyone starts thinking they're going to get richer and richer forever and ever.

Chemicals like dopamine and serotonin flood the brain, stimulating the pleasure center and suppressing our ability to think clearly. At the same time, Hollywood is pumping out a steady stream of fairy stories convincing us that... yes, true love can last a lifetime.

When the dream breaks, as one day it must, it's going to hurt – big time. That's why, when I walked into a shop in Mill Valley, California, with a new girlfriend in the first flush of a love affair, the thirty-something female sales assistant took one look at us, exclaimed "Oh my god, you're in love!" She put two fingers together in the sign of a cross in front of her, as if warding off evil spirits. She knew the pain that would follow... and she was right.

But, for me, that's no reason to avoid love. We just need to be strong enough to take the hit when it comes and to remember, as we roll around in agony on the floor, holding our stomachs to numb the aching void inside, that it's going to pass.

It's because love affairs end in suffering that we tend to think there's something wrong and blame the other partner, but in fact it's nobody's fault.

"The very nature of relationship is that it turns sour at a certain point," commented Osho, in one of his many discourses on the subject. "Both partners feel frustrated and both try to throw the responsibility on the other, so that instead of love, fighting becomes their only relationship.

     Anand Subhuti

"The problem is that the man or the woman goes on clinging even though everything is going towards hell. It is better to be miserable, but with somebody, than to be lonely, because when you are lonely you have to face yourself."

Now, you may think a spiritual seeker devoted to meditation has no time to waste in love relationships. But you are wrong – at least as far as Osho's sannyasins are concerned. In fact, Osho himself encouraged it.

This makes him an exception to a very ancient rule, setting Osho apart from almost every spiritual tradition. Historically speaking, mystics have given sex, love and women a bum rap and run away from all three, hiding in monasteries, ashrams, or caves in the Himalayas. Not without reason. They found introspection impossible in a world filled with temptation.

Osho took the opposite view: get lost in temptation deeply enough, often enough, and you'll understand its impermanence – none of it lasts. Then you might look for something more timeless and eternal.

I loved his critique of Gautam Buddha's instruction to his *bhikkhus* not to look at women: "If it had been me," said Osho, "I'd have given them a magnifying glass." In other words, don't look away, because that will only activate your imagination and lust more strongly. Rather, look more closely. Then you'll see the limitations, the imperfections, the pimples, make-up, hair dye, botox lips, plucked eyebrows... in short, the transient nature of attraction.

Here, for a moment, Shakespeare and Osho see eye to eye. One of Will's most famous sonnets, dedicated to his mysterious 'Dark Lady' mistress, is actually a spoof of classical romantic poetry, using metaphors of nature's splendour not to praise her beauty – as was the fashion – but to mark her ordinariness; the Bard's point being that he loved her anyway:

> My mistress' eyes are nothing like the sun;
> Coral is far more red than her lips' red;
> If snow be white, why then her breasts are dun;
> If hairs be wires, black wires grow on her head.
> I have seen roses damask'd, red and white,
> But no such roses see I in her cheeks;
> And in some perfumes is there more delight
> Than in the breath that from my mistress reeks...

For centuries, the identity of the 'Dark Lady' has remained a source of intense literary speculation, but an historical detective recently identified her as Aline Florio, the faithless wife of an Italian translator, working in London. When the real woman is exposed, the 'Dark Lady' fantasy evaporates, which proves what I'm saying: the plain facts of love are less interesting than the air of romantic mystery that traditionally surrounds them.

However, it needs a lot of intelligence to give up the search for a soul mate, even in old age, when a man's testosterone levels are sinking faster than real estate prices in a subprime mortgage crisis.

One has only to see a movie like *Last Chance Harvey* to understand our longing for togetherness. As the storyline develops, we watch in hopeful suspense as a burned-out American advertising executive called Harvey Shine, played by 72-year-old Dustin Hoffman, seeks a fresh start in the company of disillusioned British airport employee Kate Walker, played by 50-year-old Emma Thompson.

Oozing talent, Hoffman and Thompson manage to

pull off this otherwise corny romance, although judging by Harvey Shine's chronic heart condition, his new-found love will soon find herself in the role of nursemaid and caretaker, rather than a lover who enjoys walking around London with him.

We all know how difficult it is to be alone. Classic serial marriage addicts like Elizabeth Taylor (eight times) and Zsa Zsa Gabor (nine times) have made the record books, but it's not just a girl thing. The personal lives of Tom Cruise, Paul McCartney and John Cleese all demonstrate – if proof were needed – how men, as well as women, can't really cope unless they have someone to 'be there' for them.

As I mentioned earlier, biochemistry doesn't help and it's not just the dopamine and serotonin. Now researchers at the University of Virginia, studying MRI brain scans, tell us that lovers and close friends become entwined at a neural level. "It's essentially a breakdown of self and other; our self comes to include the people we become close to," stated one brain researcher. No wonder it hurts so much when the need arises to become two separate people once more.

But it is churlish of me to dwell on such unfriendly realities. This is no time for bad news. This is a time for love. So, let us forget about such sobering and chilly truths as aloneness, meditation and the transient nature of human relationships. Let us rather melt with warm-hearted empathy as a young couple dance on stage to a romantic song:

> *There is a country far away,*
> *There is a land far away and lost...*

Ophelia is in love with Hamlet, and he with her. In this moment, time stops. The past has dropped away. The future does not exist. In this moment, they are one.

Can their love survive the stormy seas ahead? What about Queen Elizabeth's demand for a tragic ending? What about Will Shakespeare's determination to avoid having his head removed from his shoulders? How can all of this be reconciled?

Let's see...

           Anand Subhuti

Chapter Eighteen

In The Name of the Father

Hamlet's Father's Ghost:
If thou didst ever thy dear father love,
Revenge his foul and most unnatural murder.

Hamlet:
Thy commandment all alone shall live,
Within the book and volume of my brain.

You must excuse me for returning to the subject of Elsinore's kingly ghost, but I cannot forgive Hamlet for being so spineless. He behaved as if he was nothing more than an extension of his father's ego. His father wanted revenge but, being somewhat handicapped as an insubstantial phantom, he ordered his son to do the job.

Still, the old man could have had a go at it himself. After all, if he could appear before his son and before the ordinary soldiers in the castle, why could he not appear in front of his brother, King Claudius? Why could he not torture the new king every night with his ghostly presence? Why couldn't he stand in front of his former wife, Queen Gertrude, and say "Boo!" every time she tried to enter the king's chamber? Why couldn't he sit on the bed while they were making love – after all, there's nothing more guaranteed to make a guy lose his erection than the sudden appearance of a ghost between the sheets.

But no, he asked his poor son to do the job for him and Hamlet instantly agreed. If it had been me facing that miserable paternalistic apparition, I'd have told the ghost to do his own dirty work and invited Ophelia on an extended vacation. Either that, or catch the next Viking ship to America.

Just as an historical aside, I was recently informed by a Shakespeare buff that Will himself played the ghost in Hamlet at the Globe Theatre. The role, it seems, was close to his heart, which makes me wonder how the Bard's own son, Hamnet, would have turned out, reared by such a parent. But, alas, the young man died when he was 14 years old, so we shall never know if he was shaping up to be a wimp, like his near-namesake, Hamlet.

Even Ophelia had more guts than her boyfriend. She was ready to defy her father, Polonius, and her brother, Laertes, in order to marry Hamlet.

I tell you, this habit of obedience to our fathers is driving us all nuts. Make no mistake, our fathers have betrayed us and they have betrayed this beautiful planet on which we live. They deserve to be condemned, not obeyed. They should be ridiculed, not respected.

If this sounds unfair, just think for a moment: who has given us the framework of beliefs by which we live? Who has created a society that turns us into economic slaves? Who has made us so poor in spirit that we need to run madly after material wealth? Who has told us to believe in an angry father figure in the sky who will punish us with eternal damnation if we dare to disobey?

Who but our fathers?

Perhaps we should forgive our biological fathers. Poor guys. They really didn't have a clue how they were being manipulated. My own father worked as a bank clerk for most of his life, relying on alcohol to get him through the mind-numbing activity of looking after other people's money.

But it's interesting to see how our early dependence on our fathers, as small children, has been used as a surgical social tool to castrate us. Because, you see, we were never allowed to grow up. That would have been too much of a risk for those who benefit from our immaturity.

This reminds me of Joseph Ratzinger, who, until his resignation in 2013, was the Catholic Church's earthly representative of Our Father in Heaven. By the way, just as a theatrical aside, the word 'pope', as most people know, is derived from the Greek word *pappas*, meaning 'father' and every Catholic priest is also to be addressed as 'father'. It's a simple and effective way of manipulating people by turning them into children, or worse, into a flock of sheep, cared for by the Divine Shepherd.

You see the point? As long as we think we need fathers, we reduce ourselves to children, to lesser beings. That's why I say our fathers betrayed us. They did not teach us to be independent and strong; they taught us to obey authority. They did not teach us to be intelligent; they taught us to believe what we were told. And if someone like Osho comes along to point out the absurdity of the situation, he automatically puts himself in danger.

Ratzinger identified Osho as an enemy of the church while working as a cardinal under Pope John Paul II.

Osho's irreverent description of Jesus Christ as a four-foot hunchback in need of psychological treatment, his dismissal of the Holy Trinity – Father, Son and Holy Ghost – as a 'gay trio' and his labelling of John Paul II as 'the Polak Pope' all marked him for special treatment.

One might argue that it's not polite of Osho to say such things. But how else is a compassionate mystic supposed to help people grow up, other than poking fun at the authority figures we worship? He was just doing his job.

According to an Indian journalist with close connections to the Vatican, Ratzinger was the driving force behind the campaign against Osho, which began in earnest when the mystic travelled to America in 1981. And I have to say that, for Ratzinger, the timing couldn't have been better.

Let me paint this brief picture of the international political landscape at the time (some of this info is in My Dance with a Madman, so I'll keep it short):

Newly-elected President Ronald Reagan was a gung-ho, *better-dead-than-red* anti-communist, and immediately cultivated close ties with Pope John Paul II, believing that together they could foment social unrest in Poland, which was the pope's home country, and in this way destabilize the Soviet Empire.

They needn't have bothered. Comrade Mikhail Gorbachev, in an attempt to reform the Soviet economy, inadvertently triggered a process that destroyed the Soviet Union itself. To me, it's one of those ironies of history that the first Soviet leader to be born after the Great October Socialist Revolution of 1917 was also the last Soviet leader and, indeed, the nemesis of the Socialist Revolution.

If those old Bolsheviks could have seen it coming, they would have shot Gorbachev's father and mother to prevent his conception. And if they'd seen him shaking hands with Ronald Reagan at the 1985 Geneva Summit, they'd have whispered in V.I. Lenin's mummified ear, "Comrade, the dictatorship of the proletariat has just been sold to the Coca-Cola Company."

Meanwhile, back in Rome, Ratzinger had been promoted to Head of the Inquisition, or, to give an old job its new title, Prefect of the Congregation for the Doctrine of the Faith. With direct access to Pope John Paul II and close ties to Washington, it was easy for him to urge the Reagan Administration to use all possible means to get Osho out of the USA and back to India.

Mind you, Reagan didn't need much urging. Anyone who referred to him as a 'third-rate cowboy actor' – as Osho frequently did – was likely to face a showdown at high noon. And so it turned out. Osho was arrested, jailed, framed and deported. That's the price he paid for challenging the dominant paradigm and trying to loosen its authoritarian grip on our collective psyche.

A few hundred years earlier, when Shakespeare wrote his plays, there was no father figure on the throne of England. Rather, it was a mother figure in the shape of Queen Elizabeth.

Psychologically speaking, this is a bit more tricky to handle.

When a father wields authority it's usually obvious and backed by physical force: "Do as you're told, or else..." But when a mother has power, her authority is mixed with feelings of love and care as well as discipline, which, from a child's point of view, makes it confusing.

When Margaret Thatcher died in 2013, a former member of her Cabinet, reminiscing in a television interview, said something very significant about working with Britain's first woman Prime Minister. He explained that all of Thatcher's Cabinet ministers were male and most of them had been sent to private boarding schools as children, where the only female figure was Matron, who was supposed to look after the children's general health and welfare in a 'firm but fair' way.

"Margaret was Matron and we became her wards," confided the ex-minister.

Now let's hop across the English Channel for a moment and consider the highly successful political career of Angela Merkel: Chancellor of Germany since 2005, de facto leader of the European Union and rated by Forbes magazine as the world's second-most powerful person – the highest ranking ever achieved by a woman.

At the time of writing this book, Merkel has just won another election and is heading for a third term in office. What nickname has the public given her? 'Mutti,' which is a familiar German form of 'mother' – in other words 'mummy', or if, like me, you've watched too many American movies, 'mom'. In these times of economic uncertainty, the German people like the feeling that mom is holding their hands.

Our need for parental permission manifests in many ways. Take, for example, a touchingly sensitive movie released last year titled *The Sessions*, starring John Hawkes, Helen Hunt and William Macy. As a man crippled by polio, Hawke's character seeks spiritual guidance from his local priest, played by Macy, asking him if it would be a sin to lose his virginity without being married, using a surrogate sex worker (played by Hunt).

For a moment, the priest silently communes with his divine employer, then reassures the crippled man, "In

     Anand Subhuti

my heart, I feel he'll give you a free pass on this one." So the man in the iron lung gets a green light to fuck out of wedlock.

The moment looks good onscreen and both Hawkes and Macy play their parts well, but the underlying implication disturbed me. It was saying, in effect, that we lack the maturity and intelligence to determine what's good for ourselves. We cannot act, even in our own best interests, without permission from a higher authority.

By the way, it's not my intention to single out Roman Catholicism as if it's the only culprit. The Vatican provides interesting examples, but the syndrome goes far wider.

When I first arrived in Pune and started listening to Osho's discourses, I couldn't understand why he spent so much time attacking established religion. To me, it seemed boring and irrelevant. I'd dropped religion years ago, so had many others, so why was he bothering to attack the Pope, Mother Teresa, Jesus, Moses and all the rest of that dreary company?

It wasn't until I started meditating, peering under the lid of my own psychology, that I realised how many life-negative attitudes I'd absorbed from religious faith. My parents weren't practising Christians, but I got the morality anyway, digesting it at a subliminal level along with my Kellog's Cornflakes and Shredded Wheat: don't allow yourself to really live, don't step outside the sheep pen, don't think for yourself, don't explore your sexual energy...

It took me quite a while to repair the damage. That's why I condemn Hamlet for being such a wimp. Up to the time I became a sannyasin, it was the story of my own life, too, getting caught in complex intellectual ideas about the meaning of life when the real thing – my own life energy – was suppressed, waiting to burst out from within my own body, heart and soul.

Hamlet, old chap, it's not about wondering whether 'to be or not to be'. It's about getting real.

How do you do that? Well, try this little therapeutic exercise:

Imagine you are Hamlet. You have met your father's ghost on the castle ramparts. You listen carefully to his hard luck story and you understand that you don't need to take responsibility for his problems. When he has finished talking, you look into his ghostly eyes and slowly and deliberately say the following words: "Fuck off, asshole! Do your own dirty work. I'm taking the next flight to India with Ophelia."

You won't go mad. Trust me.

     Anand Subhuti

Chapter Nineteen

All's Well That Ends Well

$\mathcal{I}$ almost forgot to tell you. The biggest drama on the opening night didn't happen onstage. It happened outside the theatre when the Pune police arrived and suddenly told us we couldn't put on the play.

It was a last-minute glitch of massive proportions. The audience was already seated. The actors had put on their make-up and were fully costumed. The radio mics had been tested and our technicians were in the control box, waiting to hit the lights and turn up the volume. Then Ragni, my co-producer, looking incredibly elegant and feminine in her evening sari, came to give me the bad news: the cops were shutting us down.

We'd put up the cash and rolled the production, only to hit a roadblock seconds before curtain up. I had to walk onto the stage, in my Shakespeare costume and announce, "There's been a slight bureaucratic hitch that's preventing us from starting the play. If you'll excuse me, I'll go out front and try to solve the problem. Meanwhile, just relax and enjoy the music."

We put on a CD of Indian music and then I joined Ragni

outside the theatre, where a Sikh police officer, looking smart in his blue, colour-coordinated shirt, tie and turban, was speaking rapidly into a large walkie-talkie handset, conversing with the shopping mall's management.

Seeing me in my puffy pantaloons and Elizabethan jacket, he gave me a quick, embarrassed smile, but continued jabbering into his oversized mobile.

So, what was the problem? Several types of official permission are required for putting on plays in Indian cities, including an okay from the Police Commissioner and the Charities Commissioner. We knew this. We'd received the double-okay at the very last minute after realizing that our friendly neighbourhood agent in Koregaon Park, who was supposed to take care of it – "Yes, yes, it's happening, by tomorrow, don't worry" – hadn't actually done anything.

It was a close shave, but Ragni shifted into high gear and with a lot of running around and fast talking she managed to obtain both permits a few hours before curtain up on the opening night. Situation sorted.

But that wasn't enough. When he got off his walkie-talkie, the police inspector told me apologetically: "Sorry to say, sir, government regulations state that special Home Ministry permission is an absolute necessity for foreigners to perform in this country... absolute necessity... *absolute necessity...absolute...*"

He was on a loop, but it was a key phrase and basically he was right. It was the rule. It was something we didn't know and hadn't figured.

The owners of the shopping mall agreed with the cops. They were on the phone to Ragni, telling her they, too, wouldn't permit the show to go ahead without police clearance on all points – it was in the contract we'd signed

     Anand Subhuti

with them. Strange. I didn't recall signing any contract and neither did Ragni. She signed a cheque for the rent and that was all. But to tell you the truth, both of us had been so busy putting on the play we couldn't remember if we'd signed anything – not a very businesslike attitude, I'm sure you'll agree.

We knew there was zero chance of obtaining Home Ministry permission to save the show, even if we flew to New Delhi with the speed of a Concorde jetliner. But the police and the managers were adamant we couldn't begin without it.

What to do? Silencing her mobile for a moment, Ragni looked at me, grimacing and smiling at the same time, indicating the challenge both frustrated and amused her. "There *must* be a way around this. In this country there's *always* a solution," she declared determinedly.

As it turned out, the police were easier to handle than the mall managers. The classic, time-honoured method of *baksheesh* took care of the inspector's requirements and I didn't really mind handing over ten thousand rupees – I'd lost so much money on this show, another couple of hundred bucks didn't make much difference.

But the mall owners were still blocking us, raising fears that they would be heavily fined by the government if ever the news got out that they'd allowed foreigners to perform without permission. And, no, they weren't interested in *baksheesh* – as I said, the owner was the wife of a gasoline king and she was loaded.

Ragni got back on her Galaxy, arguing fiercely with the management and after a long time her shoulders seemed to relax so I got the feeling something might be working. Eventually, she ended the negotiation and told me, "They're willing to let the show proceed, providing we sign a letter, drafted by them, guaranteeing we will pay any fines imposed by the Home Ministry," she informed me, then added, "Not just fines imposed on us, but also fines imposed on the mall."

No problem for this playwright. Theoretical fines for hypothetical offences imposed by invisible bureaucrats at some imaginary future date didn't worry me. I was ready to sign anything and go to debtor's prison later if necessary. All I wanted was to roll.

"Let's go for it," I said and she agreed.

For a moment, it seemed like we had a green light. But then Ragni's cell phone played its Bollywood tune and she raised a hand to stop me.

"Now what?" I asked.

"We can't start until we've signed the letter..." she reported, grimacing in frustration once more.

"My god, how long is that going to take?" I wondered, but neither of us knew the answer.

Another ten minutes passed. No sign of any letter emerging from the mall's main office. Out of the corner of my eye, I saw a member of the audience coming out of the theatre and walking away. Later, I found out she was going to buy a bottle of water and was coming back, but at the moment I suddenly feared a mass walkout by an impatient audience.

I grabbed Ragni's mobile and screamed, "Look, people are leaving the theatre! We have to start the show now... NOW!" then handed the phone back to Ragni. Another fierce conversation in Hindi ensued.

"Okay, if I wait here to sign the letter, you can start the show," she told me. I think she spent the entire evening

     Anand Subhuti

outside the theatre, waiting for the letter to come, and didn't see our performance until the second night.

As I went into the amphitheatre, my reappearance raised a cheer from the good-natured sannyasin audience, all of whom understood – some, no doubt, from personal experience – that in this country bureaucratic intervention can abruptly derail any event at any moment.

Minutes later the Prologue walked out onto the stage, unrolled his parchment and began:

> *The mark of greatness as we know*
> *Is left for history to bestow…*

After we had run the play successfully for two nights, Ragni and I sat down and drafted a letter to the Home Ministry in Delhi, seeking clarification.

We explained that, in our understanding, amateur actors from abroad who donate their services voluntarily, without being paid, need not apply to the Home Ministry for permission to perform in India – only professional performers need do that.

We asked the Home Ministry if our understanding was correct. So far, after three months of waiting, we have yet to receive a reply. There's an upside to the delay: as yet, no massive fines have been imposed on us, nor on the shopping mall, for what occurred.

Indian bureaucracy can drive you crazy if you want something. But if you don't want something – like a fine, or an embargo, for example – then, truly, it becomes a blessing. In this country, the hidden spirit of non-doing lives on, especially in government offices.

Long may it continue.

Chapter Twenty

A Thrilling Finale

*F*or one brief, shining moment, it looks as though true love is here to stay. Hamlet dances with Ophelia, Will Shakespeare dances with his wife, then they all join hands and dance together in harmony. What more could an incurable romantic wish for?

But then Will remembers the Queen's threat and, after a moment's hesitation, rudely breaks away from the other dancers, signalling for the music to cease.

"Stop! Stop!" he cries. "All this romantic nonsense... it just won't do!"

Of course, he feels bad about being a party pooper, but he's also a pragmatist. He knows what needs to be done to save his skin. He stalks back to his seat, picks up his quill pen and gets on with it.

Meanwhile, Hamlet is a changed man, open to an entirely different future. Wonderingly, he looks at Ophelia and Mrs Shakespeare and asks them, "What happens now?"

Mrs Shakespeare has the answer: "Well, if you take my advice you'll both get out of Denmark as quickly as possible. It's such a miserable country. Why don't you go to India for the winter?"

Ophelia likes this new turn of events. "India! That sounds like a wonderful idea!" she exclaims. She is a romantically inclined young woman and the promise of travelling to such an exotic country with her beloved sounds too good to be true.

Hamlet, however, has doubts. "My god, but from Elizabethan England it will us take six months just to get there!" he objects.

Mrs Shakespeare has all the answers. Pulling a couple of airline tickets from her copious bosom, she tells them, "No, no. I happen to know that Jet Airways is offering special flights from sixteenth century London nonstop to Mumbai. Look, here are the tickets. Now run along both of you."

Okay, let's back up a bit and take a look at this new development. First of all, as you may have noticed, Mrs Shakespeare is talking as if this young couple is living in Denmark, while giving them flight tickets from London. It's a question of parallel realities. In the play within the play, they are in Elsinore Castle. As Elizabethan actors they are in London. I'm comfortable with the paradox.

As for Denmark, I admit, I'm being too hard. It's not *such* a miserable country. As I said earlier, I've been going there every summer to live in a small sannyasin community, located in the countryside in Jutland – not far from where the legendary hero Amleth skewered his treacherous uncle with his sword.

When the sun shines and the temperature creeps above 20 degrees Celsius, Denmark is transformed into a paradise on earth. But, unfortunately, that tends not to happen very often, which is why I'm happy to spend a few weeks on the beaches of Goa every winter before heading for Jutland. I'm filling up my personal sunshine quota, just in case.

News of Denmark's bad weather has spread across the internet, inspiring one cynical guy to spoof a web-search failure notice: *Error 404: Danish summer not found – try Thailand.*

Another humourist posted three photos on *Facebook*:

First photo: a man and a boy are sitting on a park bench in their winter coats. The man asks the boy "When does Spring come?"

Second photo: the boy looks at the man with sad, tear-filled eyes and replies, "I live in Denmark."

Third photo: They embrace wordlessly, sharing a deep understanding of the hopelessness of the situation.

And then, of course, when summer ends and autumn begins, when the nights grow longer and darker and the temperature sinks toward zero... then it's definitely time to get out. I can't live in a country where daybreak comes at ten o'clock in the morning and nightfall arrives at four in the afternoon.

So Mrs Shakespeare has my sympathy in recommending a trip to India. By the way, when I first wrote this scene, the tickets mentioned in the dialogue were for Kingfisher Airlines, but, alas, the company went bust last year. Now it's Air India, Jet Airways, or British Airways.

The young couple are about to leave the stage to begin their journey, when Will, who's been pretending to write but was actually listening to all this, jumps to his feet.

"Wait! Hold everything!" he commands.

"Uh-oh," murmurs Mrs Shakespeare. She was hoping to

get the couple safely away before her husband interfered. Fat chance, especially when the guy playing the part is also writing the script.

Will strolls with deliberate slowness towards his wife and with forced politeness enquires, "May I have a word with you... dear?"

Mrs Shakespeare tells Hamlet and Ophelia to wait a moment and comes close to her husband, smiling brightly with an expression of pure innocence on her face, as if nothing could possibly be the matter.

"Yes, dear?"

Will puts an affectionate hand on his wife's shoulder. He is, after all, human, and wants her to know it.

"Listen, beloved," he tells her. "I know you have good intentions and you want these young people to be happy, but if they don't die, I will. The Queen has threatened me with execution if this play does not end in tragedy."

This is news to Mr Shakespeare. "Ooooh, that nasty woman!" she cries, but then inspiration strikes once more: "Wait... I know..." she pulls two more Jet Airways tickets from her bosom. "We'll all fly to India... right now, before she finds out."

Okay, never mind the implausibility of introducing airlines into an Elizabethan drama. We are approaching a significant moment, because there is only one thing preventing Will Shakespeare from agreeing with his wife and leaving this tortured situation. One tiny three-letter word called 'ego'.

Will folds his arms, looks at his wife indignantly and declares, "What? You want me to give up being the greatest playwright in England... just like that?" He snaps his fingers to emphasise the point.

Mrs Shakespeare looks at him with a mixture of pity and understanding.

"Oh, I forgot. You haven't learned how *not to be*, have you?"

Far from feeling hurt by her comment, Will agrees.

"No, indeed. Nor will I ever do so. My name is going to be remembered for centuries and centuries."

So, here we are, looking at the classic human condition in which a wonderful, juicy and exciting course of action is prohibited because of considerations of reputation, social image and personal prestige.

Just think for a moment: how many times have you felt an impulse to do something enjoyable, fun, life-enhancing, and prevented yourself because of your 'reputation' and what other people might think?

I'm reminded of one such moment in Marilyn Monroe's life. She was filming *The Prince and the Showgirl* in London and suffering immensely from the British stiff upper lips surrounding her. It wasn't only Laurence Olivier, the director, who was giving her a hard time (mainly because he wasn't able to seduce her). The stage crews at Pinewood Studios had perfected the art of inverted snobbery – pretending not to feel inferior to the film stars with whom they worked – so they ignored her and virtually cut her dead.

Of course, she should never have agreed to go there. Already deeply insecure about her acting abilities, Monroe, with her unerring sense of self-destruction, put herself in a situation that was guaranteed to make it ten times worse.

Anyway, one day Marilyn figured she'd had enough and ran off with a young man called Colin Clark, who was personal assistant to Sir Laurence (and who subsequently

     Anand Subhuti

wrote a book about his experiences). Clark and Monroe had a great time, touring Windsor Castle, walking in the fields and swimming in the River Thames. Ecstatic at being freed from the stuffy atmosphere at Pinewood, Marilyn exclaimed, "This is reality!"

Clark instantly corrected her, reminding the megastar sex symbol that the 'real world' lay in the film studios, in her movie career and in her difficult marriage with playwright Arthur Miller.

But here's my point: Clark was wrong. Both worlds were equally real and Marilyn was free to choose either one. She could have opted for the simple life, free from the pressures of being a popular actress. She could've run away with Clark, right then and there, and never looked back. What made her return to Pinewood was her investment in being a star – a totally understandable decision, but one that would ultimately destroy her.

I'm not saying Marilyn *should* have stayed with Clark. I'm saying the exhilaration she experienced with him happened because – for a few precious hours – she was leaving her image, her reputation and therefore all her insecurity and anxiety behind.

That's a choice we all make. Will's dilemma is one that faces us all, almost every day of our lives.

But Mrs Shakespeare hasn't given up on the situation. Taking her husband by the arm, she leads him to where Hamlet and Ophelia are standing. She knows that, somewhere beneath his overweening ambition, her husband has a soft heart and she appeals to it now.

"Will, love, come here," she says gently. "Look at these beautiful young people. They've just discovered the joy of living. Do you want to take it away from them?"

Confronted by the dire consequences of his script, Will hesitates.

"Well, er..." For the first time, his resolve weakens and he just doesn't know what to do.

Ta-tata-taaaaaaa!

Fanfare of trumpets and Queen Elizabeth herself comes sweeping onto the stage, accompanied by two attendants carrying swords.

"Off with their heads!" she cries in a wonderful imitation of the foul-tempered Queen of Hearts in *Alice in Wonderland*.

Will is down on his knees in a second.

"Why are these young people not yet dying or dead?" she demands imperiously.

Immediately, the Bard suppresses whatever feelings he had for the lovers and succumbs to the necessity of *realpolitik* – in other words, the ignoble art of kissing ass.

"Soon, soon, Your Majesty. I'm just about to kill them," he assures her.

But the Queen will not brook any further delay. She is determined to see heads rolling on the floor this instant.

"Do it now. I command it! Off with their heads!"

"Yes, Your Majesty," he says humbly, then turning to the young couple he apologises for what is about to happen: "I'm sorry, both of you. A thousand pardons, but it is your destiny to die in my play."

However, as I mentioned earlier, I like happy endings and so, at this critical moment, a strange and macabre figure with a skull-like head and black cape enters on the scene. Standing dramatically among the players, this ghastly apparition points an accusing finger at the Queen.

     Anand Subhuti

"Your time has come, Your Majesty," booms the figure in a hollow, ghostly voice.

The Queen is terrified. After all, it's all very well chopping off the heads of other people, but it's a different matter when it's your turn to face the Grim Reaper.

"Eeeek! Oh god! Who are you, pray?" she cries, almost fainting in alarm.

"I am the Angel of Death. And it is your time to die!" booms the voice.

The Queen clutches at her heart and staggers to one side. "Ah, it is true!" she gasps. "My heart is giving out! It is my time! Farewell, cruel world! Farewell!"

Pushing melodrama to the max and going beyond even Bollywood-style histrionics, she falls back into the arms of her attendance and is half carried, half staggers, across the stage, repeating loudly "I die! I die! I die...!"

Finally, when she's gone, the strange figure whips off its disguise to reveal the perpetrator of this eleventh-hour rescue operation: Nobody.

Nobody is immensely satisfied with her own performance and thinks Will Shakespeare should be, too. "That was pretty good acting, eh Will?" she asks.

Will is astonished. He's never seen this character before and doesn't know what she's doing in his play. "Well, obviously the queen thought so; she's dying of fright," he replies. "Who are you?"

"I'll tell you later. But first, we must find a way to end this play properly," pronounces Nobody.

In one movement, Ophelia, Hamlet and Mrs Shakespeare turned towards Will and in a single voice demand, "A *happy* ending!"

But, even with the queen off his back, Will isn't ready to agree.

"No. I refuse to write a happy ending," he tells them, stubbornly.

Nobody is genuinely puzzled. "But why?" she asks him.

"It's so ordinary, so predictable," he explains and gesturing towards the audience continues, "Look at this sophisticated audience. You can't expect them to take me seriously as a playwright if I write a happy ending."

I love pulling in the audience unexpectedly, like this, and it works well in a play where I'm free to time-jump from Elizabethan England to the present day. It also reminds everyone – as I've said before – that comedy isn't respected as much as tragedy.

However, if Will can be stubborn, so can his wife. Folding her arms in a gesture of defiance, she tells her husband, "Well, we refuse to take part in a tragic ending."

Hamlet and Ophelia immediately take her side. "Right!" They've had quite enough gloom in their lives and here they draw the line. It looks like a stand-off, but then Nobody comes up with a possible solution.

"I know," she says. "How about a thriller?"

"A thrilling ending, yes!" agrees Mrs Shakespeare, immediately enjoying the idea.

Will is flummoxed. "But I've never, ever, written a thriller," he objects.

Historically speaking, this is perfectly true. All of Shakespeare's plays contain dramatic tension, that's obvious; you can't put a story on stage without injecting some... er... well... *drama*. But he's never been one for nail-biting, fast-moving action like, for example, the kind of thing you find in *The Matrix*, or *The Terminator*. It's not his thing. There needs to be time for soliloquy, for lengthy poetic reflections

Anand Subhuti

on the deeper issues with which humanity wrestles.

Nobody has the solution. "It's easy. Listen, Will...," she whispers in his ear and slowly a smile creeps across Shakespeare's hitherto worried face.

"Okay. I'll try it," he agrees." Take your places everyone!"

The lights dim, the atmosphere on stage becomes spooky, a familiar tune begins to play and Shakespeare starts to lip sync Michael Jackson's famous number *Thriller*:

It's after midnight... and something evil's lurking in the dark...

Behind him, the rest of the cast begin the classic zombie shuffle, staring vacantly towards the audience, twitching robotically back and forth. Then everyone suddenly breaks into a synchronised high-stepping chorus, with hands raised like claws, and the audience cracks up:

It's just a thriller... thriller night...

As you can see, we're throwing caution to the winds, here, as far as paying royalties is concerned, because you just cannot find a substitute for *Thriller*. In this context, nothing else works. As with *Gangnam Style*, earlier in the tale, we will have to spend serious money if this show ever goes commercial.

As far as my own performance was concerned, it took me a while to learn the moves from Michael Jackson's video and I wouldn't say my 67-year-old body has the suppleness which the King of Pop's rubbery athletics demand. But we're all moving well, going great guns and are about two thirds of the way through the song when...

Ta-tata-taaaaaaa!

A royal fanfare interrupts our dance, announcing the return of the grim and malevolent Queen Elizabeth. She's not dead? *Oh shit.*

Chapter Twenty One

No Business Like It

I need a new ending for my play. The one I've written works fine for sannyasins and people who know Osho, but I'd like to widen it to include everyone who's interested in discovering more about themselves. After all, meditation is nobody's copyright – on the contrary, it is everybody's birthright.

The bottom line of spiritual growth is: you need to find your own buddha nature. It's helpful to hook up with spiritual masters like Osho and other people who teach meditation, but this doesn't absolve you from responsibility.

As far as I'm concerned, anyone who has touched the inner core of Buddha nature can write his, or her, own ending to my play. However, there is one condition on which I must insist: all the characters need to end up in India.

Even though this country is doing its best to destroy itself as rapidly as possible, I still want Hamlet, Ophelia, Mrs Shakespeare, Will, Nobody and even Queen Elizabeth to fly Jet Airways to Mumbai or Delhi and remain in the country for at least six months.

 Anand Subhuti

Why? Because the vibe of meditation still lingers here and that's a tremendous help for people setting out on the path of spiritual enquiry. I say 'spiritual' but it's a misleading term. Really, I'm referring to anybody who begins to understand that, even though we seem to be awake – walking, talking, acting normally – we are afflicted by a pernicious sleep that keeps the whole of humanity drugged.

You want to know the truth? Take a look at Michael Jackson's *Thriller* video, not at the man himself but the guys who dance with him. Yep, that's us. We are walking zombies, obeying a program of unthinking social conformity that has been hard-wired into our brains.

Never mind who did it. You can blame our fathers, our mothers. You can blame the Queen of England, Wills and Kate, the Vatican, the US Reserve Bank, the Illumminati, the Russian mafia, Exxon, Monsanto, Calvin Klein... it really doesn't matter who benefits from our 'waking sleep'. What matters is the understanding that we are, indeed, stacking *zzzzzz* in slumberland. This realization alone begins the process of waking up.

Remember, though, we're all going to face the challenge of *not to be*. Like it or not, it's unavoidable. The rules of the game clearly state that we cannot simply add meditation to our nicely polished, sophisticated personalities and get on with life as before.

That's not going to work. We need to find a way of dropping the ego, dis-identifying with personality, otherwise we may as well buy a lifetime subscription to our local couch potato club and go on watching *Strictly Come Dancing* and *The X Factor* on Saturday night television.

Now that I've widened the picture, I can tell you how

we ended *Shakespeare the Meditator* but please remember this play was performed in Pune, close to the ashram where I lived and worked for years. Moreover, at least 80 percent of the audience was made up of sannyasins. In this kind of context, the ending you're about to read makes a lot of sense. It's like an 'in-house' joke that we all enjoyed and shared.

Here we go:

You will recall that the Bard is onstage, doing a mean impersonation of Michael Jackson, dancing to the tune of *Thriller*. Then, to everyone's dismay, there is a fanfare of trumpets heralding the reappearance of Queen Elizabeth, who by now ought to have expired from heart failure.

The music stops and everyone falls to their knees as the Queen arrives with her attendants. Execution and tragedy are once again hanging in the air. But there's a difference in Good Queen Bess. She's changed. She's wearing neither her crown nor her mask. Her face looks calm and peaceful as she gazes lovingly upon her subjects and addresses them thus:

"One moment. Please don't be afraid
Of being hurt by this old maid.
If I may choose twixt life and death
I'd really rather keep my breath.
So let me join you in your gladness
And say goodbye to royal sadness."

A royal breakthrough has happened at last. The pressure is off. The young lovers are saved and Will gets to keep his head on his shoulders. All because the Queen, when taken to the verge of death, is able to understand that she really wants to be alive, and what is the use of being alive just to be miserable? Misery is a kind of death, a decision to turn away from life. Now the Queen is ready to enjoy herself.

Mrs Shakespeare is the first to congratulate her. Taking the Queen affectionately by the arm, she brings her to centre stage and confides:

"Your Majesty, I'm glad to see,
That, deep inside, you're just like me!"

Will goes over to Nobody, whom he hasn't really met until now. I'm not sure I intended it when I wrote the play, but it's kind of symbolic that the Bard connects with Nobody only at the end of the show. Up to now, Will has been clinging to his status as a famous playwright and, as his wife points out, he hasn't learned how not to be. Now the doors of understanding are beginning to open, even for him.

Will asks this mysterious stranger:

"So tell me, Master Nobody
Where is this Land of Not To Be?"

This is where the play gets a little provincial. Nobody replies:

"Well, I would have told you sooner
I found it all right here in Pune.
There's a man I came to see
He's the King of *Not to Be*."

At this point, I must call 'time-out' to take care of another paradox. As any student of philosophical logic will tell you, you cannot have a *King of Not to Be*. I studied these kinds of intellectual gymnastics as part of my university degree, so I should know. Why? Because in order to be a king you need to be somebody, which automatically prevents you from being nobody. It's basic Aristotelean syllogistic logic:

All inhabitants of the Land of Not To Be are nobodies.
A king is not a nobody.
Therefore, there cannot be a King of Not To Be.

I can't believe I wasted three years of my life studying this stuff.

Anyway, the fact is, unless you are a nobody, you have no business in the Land of Not to Be. You lack the necessary visa in your passport, allowing you to cross the border.

Fortunately, however, Aristotle's brutal grip on the Western intellect has loosened during the last couple of hundred years, not least because of the introduction of a wide range of hallucinogenic drugs at our academies of learning in the late Sixties. As one stoned fellow student once remarked to me: "Get out of your head man, check out the colours..."

Moreover, no poet worthy of the name – I count myself among them – gives a damn what the old Greek egghead thought. To me, it's legitimate to refer to Osho as the 'King of Not to Be' because, of all the spiritual teachers I know, or have read about, he is the least compromising. Lots of people teach meditation. Few attack the causes of our spiritual sleep.

But, if you really object, I have no problem with you declaring yourself as the King of Not To Be, providing that, first of all, you fulfil a simple, basic requirement: *just wake up.*

Now Mrs Shakespeare reveals she is also acquainted with Osho:

"Well, of course, I knew him well,

It's *his* business that we tell."

Will asks his wife: "What business can this be, my dear,

That fills you all with such good cheer?"

Nobody: "Well, there's no business like show business."

Mrs Shakespeare: "Or maybe we should say: there's no

Anand Subhuti

business like *O-show* business!"

Cue for a song. The entire cast lines up and sings the following words to one of the best-known tunes in the entertainment business:

> *There's no business like O-show business, like no business I know,*
>
> *Everything about it is appealing, everything your energy can do,*
>
> *Nowhere can you get that happy feeling, when you are shouting the hoo-hoo-hoo!*
>
> *There's no people like O-show people, they smile when they are low,*
>
> *Even when the chips are down and you are broke, you fly to Goa like it's a joke.*
>
> *Even when your girl is with another bloke, you go on with the show.*

As you can see, there are in-jokes in the lyrics, such as "hoo! hoo! hoo!" which refers to Osho's best-known meditation technique: Dynamic. Held at the ashram every morning at sunrise and lasting one hour, this meditation has a stage in which people jump up and down in the air, arms raised above their heads, shouting the mantra "Hoo!"

In fact, the whole first half-hour of the meditation is extremely vigorous, more like a workout at the gym. Only in the second half do the meditators become silent and still.

Once more, I need to state that if my play is ever performed as a commercial venture, I'll have to change the closing song, or pay royalties. *There's No Business Like Show Business* is a very old tune by now, but I'm pretty sure copyright still applies. We continue:

*Getting up at dawn to do Dynamic, staying up to dance
    the night away,*
*Diving deeply into meditation, Osho-connection is here
    to stay.*
*The tough relationships that you've been in, are just a
    way of finding 'Who Is In'.*

Who Is In? is the name of a three-day workshop that
invites you to look at yourself. It's based on the teachings of
Ramana Maharshi, whom I mentioned in connection with
Carl Gustav Jung in an previous chapter.

Ramana advocated asking the question 'Who am I?'
as a method self-enquiry. Osho changed the question to
'Who is in?' and suggested making it a three-day process.
Once you get the knack of it, you can use any situation in
life as an invitation to look at yourself, especially the ups
and downs of love relationships – that's the meaning of
the line.

Now we return for the final chorus:

*There's no business like O-show business, like no business
    I know,*
*Everything about it is appealing, everything your energy
    can do,*
*Nowhere can you get that happy feeling, when you are
    shouting the hoo-hoo-hoo!*
*There's no people like O-show people, they smile when
    they are low,*
*Even when the chips are down and you are broke, you fly
    to Goa like it's a joke.*
*Even when your girl is with another bloke, you go on with
    the show...*
                    (slowing down for the finale)
And... that's... the... end... of... the... show!

                    Anand Subhuti

Thunderous applause, the cast bows, curtain down.

I was happy with our performance. As I said in the beginning, the script worked well and there were no dead spots. I'd learned a great deal since staging the show the year before, noticing, for example, when some songs were too long. With a little editing, the pace picked up and I don't think there was a single moment when the audience was bored. Considering it's a spiritual play with a philosophical message, that's nothing short of a miracle.

However, you see the need to broaden the scope of the ending. The art of *not to be* isn't something that Osho discovered. It's been a constant theme in Zen for hundreds of years. In fact, it goes back to Gautam Buddha, who lived 2,500 years ago and probably even precedes him.

Likewise, the sannyasin way of life isn't something that needs to be confined to us. It can be embraced by anyone who learns to trust in the flow of life rather than mind-created theories *about* life.

So, it looks like I've got work to do. I have to write a new finale that includes Osho but goes wider. Maybe all the characters go off in search of different ways to experience themselves:

One goes for a meditation retreat to a Tibetan Buddhist monastery, such as Lamayuru in Ladakh, one does a Vipassana course with Goenka, one enrols in a yoga program in Rishikesh, one checks out new gurus like Prem Baba and Muji, and one goes to Pune to experience life in the resort.

It's just an idea. I haven't really thought it through. But, as I say, all the characters need to visit India. It's not the only place in the world where meditation can be experienced – of course not. You can experience it anywhere on this planet, wherever you are, anytime you like. Why? Because it's inside you. Just go in and find it.

But for sure, within the boundaries of the nation that calls itself India, you will find the strongest support for your self-enquiry. In this sense, India isn't really a country, but a state of consciousness.

You can't say that about Denmark, which, like most Western countries, is only just beginning to hear about meditation. In fact, when I get back to Denmark this summer, I think I'll pay another visit to Kronborg Castle and have a word with that ghost who is probably still walking the battlements. He may think, as a ghost, he's a good example of how *not to be*, but he's got it all wrong.

As you have probably guessed, this was intended to be the final chapter. But there is something more to be understood. And even though we have left the mainstream far behind and are now wandering into the borderlands of mystical revelation, straining credibility to the max, we must keep going.

We may be pushing the envelope too far, but let us take heart from the all-American viewpoint of try, try, try again:

I love that even in the toughest moments, when we're all sweating it – when we're worried that the bill won't pass, and it seems like all is lost – Barack never lets himself get distracted by the chatter and the noise. Just like his grandmother, he just keeps getting up and moving forward... with patience and wisdom, and courage and grace.

Thank you, Michelle Obama. And after all, even if you do fall on your nose, as the President has done on several occasions, it's simply proof that you're still moving forwards, otherwise you'd fall backwards and crack your skull.

Thus inspired, our journey continues...

     Anand Subhuti

Chapter Twenty Two

The Land of Not To Be

This is where it all began: in a suburb of Pune called Koregaon Park.

I used to live here in a bamboo hut. Now, I'm staying in a fancy, air-conditioned apartment, more or less at the same spot where the hut was located.

I used walk across open fields to get to the ashram. Now, I weave my way around apartment blocks, dodging traffic and inhaling exhaust fumes.

I used to wear bright orange clothes. Now, I wear street clothes most of the time, changing to a maroon-coloured robe only when I'm inside the 'Osho Meditation Resort'.

The ashram itself is still beautiful, like a small island of sanity surrounded by urban madness. The intensity has gone, because the ashram is no longer jam-packed with hundreds of sannyasins, but the quality of meditation I experience here is pretty much the same as it always was.

The winter season is coming to an end and the hot season will soon begin in earnest: mangoes, warm nights and the sound of cuckoos going crazy at dawn when they call to each other – the villagers used to say they are calling for the monsoon. In Pune, you just have time to listen to them before the sound of traffic drowns out everything.

Ragni, my co-producer, has gone to Bollywood to seek fame and fortune in the movie industry, but we may team up again some time to stage our Shakespeare play in Mumbai. And a friend of mine wants to translate the play and stage it in Germany.

With these two destinations in mind, I spend time in Pune writing the new ending. I pick up the story at the moment when Queen Elizabeth comes back from her near-death experience as a transformed woman, the lovers are saved and Will is off the hook.

It goes like this:

Will (*to Nobody*): So tell me, Master Nobody
Where is this Land of Not To Be?
Nobody: Well, if you look beyond your mind
You'll find it's been there all the time.
But meditation is more fun
If to India you come!

Curiously enough, it is the Queen who is first off the starting blocks. She seizes enthusiastically on this notion, as if, having clung grimly to the polarity of misery for so long, she can hardly wait to swing to the opposite pole and have some adventures. She's like a terminally-ill patient who thought she was ready to die and then suddenly discovers she has a bucket list to check off first.

Elizabeth: India! Oh yes, that's hip!
If my old bones can make the trip.
I think I'll go to Dharamsala
And hang out with the Dalai Lama.

Well, of course... what do you expect of a monarch? She's not going to waste her time listening to any cheap

     Anand Subhuti

bidi wallah guru. Her Royal Highness will settle for nothing less than an audience with His Holiness and we can confidently predict that the Indian press, addicted as it is to abbreviations, will emblazon its front pages with the headline "HRH Greets HH."

But there's a temporal-spatial issue. In the sixteenth century, during the reign of Good Queen Bess, the Dalai Lama was only in his third or fourth incarnation and residing in Tibet, which could conceivably render the queen's trip to Dharamshala futile. However, as you will have noticed, time seems to be very elastic in this play, so let's assume that by the time Her Majesty reaches the Dalai Lama's temple in McLeod Ganj she'll find the 14th incarnation sitting there, ready to receive her.

But it seems she won't be alone. Her attendants, having lived for so long as extensions of her Royal will, naturally assume they'll be going with her:

Attendants: Oh yes, Your Majesty, it's true
Can we come along with you?
Elizabeth (*to her Attendants*): I think it's time for you to see
You really don't belong to me.
Nobody (*to Attendants*):
Find a path that suits *you* best,
And give this 'royal' thing a rest!

Sound advice to all sheep-like followers. Now it's Mrs Shakespeare's time to come forth and shine. Having been forced by Elizabethan convention to live in the shadow of her famous playwright husband, she's more than ready to break loose and pursue her own interests at last:

Mrs Shakespeare: Yoga is what I love best.
And so I'll go to Rishikesh.
Sitting by the Ganges stream

Enjoying yoga – that's my dream!
I'll practice my *asanas* daily
Standing on my head... well, maybe.

I can picture Mrs Shakespeare in Rishikesh. There are some lovely ashrams by the Ganges and lots of yoga courses. Every morning the streets of Laxmanjula are full of slim, good-looking young Western women walking purposefully to their daily classes, with a long, thin bag slung over one shoulder containing a rolled-up yoga mat. She'll be right at home.

One word of advice, though, as a concerned husband: don't spend more than a few seconds in the *sirhasana* headstand position, my dear. It may be called the 'King of Asanas' but too much blood flooding into the brain can damage those delicate little neural networks. Spirituality does not require one to be brain dead, unless of course you're following the mainstream religions, in which case it helps a lot.

The attendants, lost without a leader, turn to Mrs Shakespeare as a substitute authority figure:

Attendants (*to Mrs S*): Oh yes we're good at yoga, too,
Perhaps we'll come along with you.
Mrs Shakespeare (*to the Attendants*): Find a method of your own
Don't just follow... stand alone.

As you can see, the attendants, who have been more or less mute throughout the show, are getting more air time. That's because they add a touch of clowning to all these possibilities opening up for the other characters. I want to keep it light, otherwise it'll come across like a *Lonely Planet* list of 'interesting places to meditate.'

Now Hamlet brings in Osho and the Pune ashram:

 Anand Subhuti

Hamlet (*to Ophelia*):
I'm sure we'll get enlightened sooner
If we meditate in Pune.
Ophelia (*alarmed*):
But isn't that the 'free love' ashram?
Will I lose my love, my passion?

Ophelia is worried, and with good reason. The ashram's track record as a graveyard for long-term relationships is impressive. The basic problem is that two people in a love partnership who come to Pune and start exploring personal growth rarely develop at the same speed.

For example, if the female partner starts doing Dynamic Meditation and emotional release work, she's going to open new energy channels inside her body, allowing all kinds of feelings to surface. She's going to feel more alive, more energized, which can be dangerous for a relationship that was moving along in a comfortable, settled routine.

Maybe the male partner is more interested in Vipassana, a slower and more traditional method of discovering one's inner world. If the initial 'hot' phase of their love relationship is over and the guy 'needs space' in order to meditate, the woman may start to feel – in the immortal words of Elizabeth Taylor – like a cat on a hot tin roof.

Moreover, lots of singles come to Pune, interested in new adventures, so, all in all, it's a pretty volatile place. Couples do come and do survive. Others, with the wisdom of experience, choose to come one at a time, while the other partner stays home and keeps his fingers crossed.

So, Ophelia's concern is well founded. Meanwhile, the attendants are seizing their chance to move in on this fair young maiden by offering their support.

1st Attendant: Don't worry, dear, we'll come with you

2nd Attendant: And sing and dance the whole night through!

Hamlet (*taking Ophelia's hand and pulling her gently away from the Attendants*):

That won't be necessary, good fellows.

We can celebrate by ourselves.

We'll go to Pune as a pair

A challenge will await us there.

Ophelia (*no longer afraid, but courageous*):

Let's see if we can both be free

And true lovers still shall be.

My feeling is they'll be okay. They are too much in love to be distracted by other dating adventures. Now it's Will's turn. What's his decision? Where will he want to go?

Will: All my life I've been a playwright

Finding words to make you say right.

So maybe I should shut up now

And silently meditate somehow.

I'll find a monastery in Ladakh

And take the pressure off my back.

1st Attendant:

Let's join the Bard in silence deep

2nd Attendant:

If it doesn't put us both to sleep.

Not much chance of that, guys, I need to tell you. Apart from a few days in August, during an all-too-brief summer, Ladakh is an extremely cold place, with sub-zero temperatures guaranteed to keep you shivering and wide awake. You'll need lots of padded layers just to stay alive.

On top of that, meditation programmes offered by Tibetan Buddhist monks usually include plenty of crashing cymbals, banging drums and loud horns. Why? Because unlike our Sunday services and sermons, they know the idea is to wake up, not fall asleep.

I have a lot of respect for Tibetan Buddhism. It's not my cup of tea, but it's an alive spiritual tradition with some remarkable leaders. I've met enough radiantly-smiling abbots in monasteries on my trips through the Himalayas to know they have a real deal going.

I recall one time, sitting in the Sakya Abode Hotel in Kaza, the capital of Spiti Valley, when a tall, elderly Tibetan monk walked gracefully through the lounge. Without thinking, my hands went into a namasté and he returned the greeting.

"Who's that?" I asked my companion, when the monk had gone.

"Him," he replied, pointing to an old black-and-white photo on the wall, showing a lama sitting grandly on a throne, somewhere in Tibet, back in the 30s. I think that's the first and only time I've seen someone in two incarnations at once.

Meanwhile, back on stage, Nobody admonishes the attendants for their attitude of slavishly following others:

Nobody (*to Attendants*):
Now stop this nonsense, both of you
Find something specially meant for you!
1st Attendant:
Okay, we'll walk the Himalayan hills
From end to end in search of thrills.
2nd Attendant:
We'll trek from Kathamanadu to Kulu
And touch the feet of every guru.
That's it. All the characters have expressed their spiritual desires and are ready to depart. Only Nobody is left, but she

is in a different category and will not be making the trip
to India. Well, let me rephrase that: Nobody will be going
to the non-geographical India that exists within us all in a
mystical sense – the place she calls the *Land of Not To Be*.

Nobody: Now I can say goodbye in style,
Let me vanish for a while.
Nobody was never here,
It's time for me to disappear.
If you wish, you can find me
In the Land of Not To Be.

The last lines go to Will. He's a changed man, ready
to give up his reputation and embark on a journey of self-
discovery, but he is, after all, a writer. He can't help it. So,
naturally, he's thinking of turning this new situation into
another play:

Will: Meet we all, here, in one year
There'll be so much for us to hear.
I'll write a new play, make amends,
Called 'Shakespeare the Meditator And His Friends'.

Cue for a closing song. Obviously, I can't use *No Business
Like O-Show Business* with the new ending. Instead, I've
chosen to repeat the opening number, using new lyrics:

Another drama for you to see,
Another story ends happily
In meditation, in ecstasy,
In the Land of Not to Be.
Another drama to make you smile,
Another story performed in style
We'll see you later, in a while,
In the Land of Not to Be.

Heroes, zeroes, kings and queens

                    Anand Subhuti

Come to India it seems.
Cleopatra longs to be
In Rishikesh with Anthony,
Juliet and Romeo
Left for Pune long ago.
Let your heart be open wide
Close your eyes and go inside.
There is more for you and me
In the Land of Not to Be.

Another drama for you to see,
Another story ends happily
In meditation, in ecstasy,
In the Land of Not to Be.
Another drama to make you smile,
Another story performed in style
We'll see you later, in a while,
In the Land of Not to Be... you gotta be there!...
In the Land of Not to Be.

Epilogue

I'd like to give the Bard the final word, but Will doesn't seem to possess the depth he needs for this occasion. You don't believe me? Listen to this lament by *Macbeth*:

```
Life's but a walking shadow, a poor player,
That struts and frets his hour upon the stage,
And then is heard no more. It is a tale
Told by an idiot, full of sound and fury,
Signifying nothing.
```

Sheer nonsense. Every human being, in his or her essence, is pure consciousness – that's our significance, our dignity, our divinity. You just need to find it. You need to start the inner journey and go looking for it. Remember, though, it's expensive. The price you need to pay is everything you think you are.

So it's hard to see how Shakespeare can provide the 'PS' to round off this little saga of being and not being.

But wait... what's this? Among all the tragedies, comedies and tragi-comedies penned by the Bard, I have found one line that will suffice to end this book. How appropriate that it was uttered by my favourite character:

"The rest is silence."

Thank you, Hamlet.

     Anand Subhuti

The complete script of

When Shakespeare
Lost the Plot

By Anand Subhuti

begins on the following
page...

Enter Prologue with scroll.

Prologue:
The mark of greatness, as we know,
Is left for history to bestow.
And who of us, now sitting here,
Will be remembered through the years?
William Shakespeare, there's a name,
Four hundred years of global fame.
His plays show man in good, in badness,
Our vanity, our pride, our madness.
The rise and fall of kings and queens,
Blind ambition, broken dreams.
Shakespeare's mighty pen described it,
What unkind critic will deny it?
But this I say, no hesitation,
Will never knew of meditation.
His busy mind was full of chatter,
He didn't think that silence mattered.
His characters did everything
But close their eyes and look within.
So come with me, let me invite you
With this small drama to excite you,
And meet Will Shakespeare and his wife
And give them both a different life.
And what we poor players lack in skill
Let your imagination now fulfill.

Queen Elizabeth walks swiftly onto the stage, followed by an attendant. Prologue becomes her second attendant. She is holding a manuscript in her hand and she is angry. William Shakespeare follows her.

Elizabeth: I will not have this play performed in my court, not while there is a single breath left in my body. No, no, no, Master Shakespeare!

Shakespeare (*protesting*): But your Majesty, it is a worthy play...

Elizabeth (*waving the papers at him*): I commanded a tragedy, Master Shakespeare.

Shakespeare: Romeo and Juliet is a tragedy, your Majesty.

Elizabeth (*shaking her head*): Ha! Do you take me for a fool?

Shakespeare: No indeed, your Majesty.

Elizabeth: It is a love story, Master Shakespeare, and what is more, it is an indecent love story! Will you have me sit on my throne, in front of the entire court, and watch while a young girl, barely 13 years old, shares her bed with her lover?

Shakespeare: But they were married, your Majesty.

Elizabeth: A hasty, secret wedding, performed against all wise counsel. It cannot excuse the scandal you will have us watch.

Shakespeare: But they both die in the end, your Majesty.

Elizabeth: Too late, Master Shakespeare, much too late! The romance has already happened. I will have none of it (*she rips up the manuscript and throws it on the floor*).

     Anand Subhuti

Shakespeare (*horrified*): My play!

He tries to gather the pieces, but the Queen stops him.

Elizabeth: Leave it there, I command you! And write me another play, to be performed in court within the week, or risk my deep displeasure. Do I make myself clear Master Shakespeare?

Shakespeare: Indeed, your Majesty, very clear.

Elizabeth: So be it. One week, Master Shakespeare. Not a day longer.

Haughtily, she starts to walk away.

Shakespeare (*to the audience*): My God, what a bitch!

Elizabeth stops, turns slowly in a menacing way towards Shakespeare.

Elizabeth: What did you say, Master Shakespeare?

Shakespeare (*realizes the Queen was still within earshot, smiles and tries desperately to avoid having his head cut off*): Er... I said... That I am rich... Your patronage prevents me... from... er... falling in a ditch.

Queen Elizabeth gives a scornful snort of contempt and leaves the stage, with her attendants. Shakespeare waits until she has gone, then starts to pick up the pieces of his torn manuscript. As she leaves, two players belonging to the same theatre company as Shakespeare come running onstage, the girl being chased by the boy, and laughing.

First Player (*approaching Shakespeare and mocking him*): How now, what grave misfortune have we here?

Second Player: Her Majesty was not too pleased, I fear!

First player: Why Will, what ails you man? Why this distress?

Second Player: Have you been fighting with our Royal Mistress?

Shakespeare: Leave me alone, good fellows, I entreat you. I lack the time and humour now to meet you.

First player picks up two of pieces of paper and hands one to her companion. They tease Will by exaggerating and over-playing the roles of Romeo and Juliet.

First Player (*playing Juliet*):
Oh Romeo, Romeo! Wherefore art thou Romeo?

Second Player (*playing Romeo*):
But soft, what light through yonder window breaks?
It is the East and Juliet is the sun!

First Player (*surrendering*):
Take me, Romeo, for I am yours!

     Anand Subhuti

Second Player (*running towards her*): My love! My
angel!

*They collapse together on the floor with giggles of
laughter.*

Shakespeare (*irritated*): Stop it, both of you! Leave
me in peace. For I must write a tragedy, within a
week.

First Player: What story will you tell? Hast thou
begun?

Shakespeare: Alas, I know not. Inspiration have I
none.

*The two players look at each other and nod
agreement.*

Second Player: Will, we can help you...

First Player: ...if you so desire.

Shakespeare: How now? What mischief do you two
conspire?

First Player: Last month, in Denmark, we played
before the king...

Second Player: In his great castle did we dance
and sing...

First Player: A mighty feast was held, with many
plays...

Second Player: Heroic tales and legends from the
grave...

First Player: One story was admired above them all...

Second Player: The greatest tragedy, wherein a king did fall...

First Player: The king's own brother did most treacherously take his life...

Second Player: And then he forced the Queen to be his wife!

Shakespeare: So far so good... and then?

First Player: Then her poor son, Hamlet, tortured by this stealth...

Second Player: Knows not whether to kill the new king, or himself...

First Player: And so he struggles on, quite desperately

Second Player: Not knowing whether to be, or not to be...

Shakespeare (*intrigued by the story*): It is a worthy tale. What happens next?

The two players look at each other and scratch their heads and look puzzled.

First Player: Er... we forget! It matters not, Will, draw upon thy skill...

Second Player: And let your clever mind write what you will.

　　　　　Anand Subhuti

First Player: Just make it up, you shall invent the rest,

Second Player: After all, it is what you do best!

First Player: As long as they all die when the play ends...

Second Player: The Queen will love you...

First Player (*rubbing fingers to indicate money*): ...and make sweet amends!

Shakespeare: It shall be done. I'll write this 'Hamlet' now.

For I must save my precious neck somehow!

Henceforth, Will Shakespeare's plays shall ever be,

Remembered for their gloom and tragedy!

All gather together for the opening song. Queen Elizabeth comes onstage with her attendants and stands separately, looking proud and aloof, and she does not sing.

Another drama for you to see,
Another ending in misery,
It's oh-so tragic, it has to be
It's for her Royal Majesty.
Another drama to make you sad,
Another story that's going bad
If you enjoy it
You must be mad!
It's for her Royal Majesty.

Heroes, zeroes, kings and villains
Kill each other with precision.
Cleopatra's destiny
Dying with Mark Anthony,
Juliet as we all know
Killed herself for Romeo,
Star-crossed lovers, heartbreak endings
Tragedy and gloom descending
Is there more that we can't see?
Is this all that's meant to be?

Another drama for you to see,
Another ending in misery,
It's oh-so tragic, it has to be
It's for her Royal Majesty.
Another drama to make you sad,
Another story that's going bad
If you enjoy it
You must be mad!
It's for her Royal Majesty... we're going crazy!...
It's for her Royal Majesty.

Actors depart, leaving Will Shakespeare (WS) sitting alone, writing with a quill pen (Attendants remain standing at the back).

WS: "To be or not to be, that is *the* question"... Yes... that is the question... (*writing*)...

Enter Shakespeare's wife (SW). She has a crochet circle in her hand. She looks at her husband, recognizing that he is completely preoccupied.

WS: "...Whether 'tis nobler in the mind..."

SW: Will dear... Will... WILL!!! Fetch another basket of firewood, there's a good fellow.

                         Anand Subhuti

WS: Er... what?

SW: Wood, dear, the fire's going out and there's a winter chill in the air today.

WS: "To suffer... the slings and arrows of outrageous fortune..." (*writing*) yes, I like that!

SW (*wearily*): Writing again, I see.

WS (*not looking up*): Hmm...

SW: Not another tragedy I hope.

WS (*frostily*): Her Majesty, Queen Elizabeth, happens to be very fond of tragedies.

SW: That's because she's old and sick and dying.

WS (*shocked, indignant and scared*): Hush, woman, hold your tongue! Such things may not be said without immediate arrest and punishment.

SW (*shrugs*): Everyone's saying it except you. The gossip is all over London that the Queen will die before the year is out.

WS: Alas, I fear it. And what will happen to our poor company of players then?

SW comes over to him, smiling and seductive.

SW: Will, sweetheart, write me a nice comedy... something to make me smile and laugh... like you used to in the old days... to please me?

WS: Dearest, I will... but not now. (*stands up*) This new play, Hamlet, is going to be my greatest triumph. The great tragedy of the young Prince of Denmark, torn between action and inaction, decision and indecision, life and death... (*dramatically with a flourish*)... "To be, or not to be, that is the question!"

SW remains unimpressed. She picks up the bucket and hands it to him.

SW: Firewood or no firewood? *That* is the question. Now get along with you or we'll both die of cold tonight.

WS (*taking the bucket*): Oh very well... But wait! I see how it must continue... (*sits down and writes furiously*) "To sleep, perchance to dream - aye, there's the rub: For in that sleep of death what dreams may come..."

SW: I give up. Give me the bucket (*picks it up*). (*addressing the audience*). Equal rights for women is going to come a little too late for me. (*smiling deviously at WS*) But I have my ways. Buy me a new dress, Will, and I'll forgive you everything."

WS (*not looking up*): Yes dear.

SW (*pleased at herself for persuading him*): Ha! (*to the audience*) You see? It's better to be. How can you wear a new dress if you choose not to be!

SW exits with her basket. An actor come onstage carrying a human skull and approaches WS. He has come to audition for the role of Hamlet. He was one of the two players who teased Will earlier, giving him the idea to write this play.

Anand Subhuti

H (*coming close to WS, he accidentally almost thrusts the skull in his face*): Excuse me, Will.

WS (*looks up, sees the skull and is frightened*): Aaaargh! For God's sake, man, what do you think you're doing?

H (*hides the skull clumsily behind his back*): Sorry, Will. I've come for the audition.

WS: What?

H: The part. I've come to play Hamlet.

WS: But why the skull?

H: Well, you said it's a tragedy, so I brought along my grandfather to add a little atmosphere.

WS: Oh, very well (*takes skull to inspect*). After all, if I fail to please the Queen, this is what I will look like in a week! (*gives him a script to read*): Let's put him down... stand here, face the audience and read this.

Hamlet strikes a very theatrical pose.

H: To be, or not to be, that is... such a stupid question! (*laughs*)

WS: What do you mean, man?

H: Nobody asks questions like this, Will.

WS: I don't believe this! You and your colleague gave me that line yourselves, from the play in Denmark!

H (*shrugs*): I guess it sounds better in Danish.

WS (*annoyed*): Just read the script.

H: ...Whether 'tis nobler in the mind to suffer
The slings and arrows of outrageous fortune,
Or to take arms against a sea of troubles,
And by opposing end them.

WS: That's better.

Enter Shakespeare's Wife, looking sceptically at Hamlet.

SW: So... let me get this straight. This handsome-looking young man is called Hamlet.

WS: Right.

SW: Hamlet's father was the King of Denmark, but he was killed by a rival. The rival becomes the new King of Denmark and marries Hamlet's mother.

WS: Right.

SW: Hamlet wants to kill the new king, to revenge his father, but instead spends a long time wondering whether to be or not to be, which makes everything very complicated. And how does it all end...?

WS: In tragedy, of course.

SW: Hamlet dies...?

WS: Yes.

     Anand Subhuti

SW: Hamlet's mother dies?

WS: Yes.

SW: The new king dies?

WS: Yes.

SW: The king's prime minister dies?

WS: Yes.

SW: The king's prime minister's son dies?

WS: Yes.

Enter Ophelia, looking dreamy and sad. She was the otherplayerwhowasteasingShakespeareinanearlier scene.

SW: And who might this young lady be?

WS: This is Ophelia, the Prime Minister's daughter. She's in love with Hamlet.

SW: Ah, something to be happy about, at last!

WS: Not exactly. You see, the murder of his father has driven Hamlet almost mad, so he rejects Ophelia. Watch and see!

H (*to Ophelia*): I did love you once.

O (*sad yet still hopeful*): Indeed, my lord, you made me believe so.

H: You should not have believed me. I loved you not.

O (*hurt and crushed*): Alas, I was the more deceived.

H: Get thee to a nunnery: why wouldst thou be a breeder of sinners?

O: O, help him, you sweet heavens! I fear that my true love is going mad!

H: Get thee to a nunnery, go: farewell. Or, if thou wilt needs marry, marry a fool; for wise men know well enough what monsters you make of them. To a nunnery, go, and quickly too. Farewell.

O: O heavenly powers, restore his troubled mind to peace and sanity!

Ophelia sinks down in despair. SW looks at the scene and moves slowly towards the couple.

SW: So Hamlet told her he loved her, and now he doesn't... and now what will she do?

WS: Er... she will throw herself in a lake.

SW: And drown herself and die?

WS: Yes, in her grief and her despair.

SW (*slowly*): Will...

WS: Hmmm...?

SW: Don't you think you're overdoing it, just a little bit? All this doom and gloom...?

WS: The Queen will love it.

SW: Yes, well, the Queen is 67 years old and still a virgin. (*goes to Ophelia*) But what about all the young women who will watch your play? "Breeder of sinners"? "Get thee to a nunnery"? What kind of example are you giving them?

WS (*wearily*): You don't understand, woman.

SW: Oh but I rather think I do... (*to Ophelia*) Come here, sweetheart.

Ophelia looks surprised.

O: Who me?

SW: Yes, dear (takes her by the hand and leads her to one side). Now listen, you're much too young to go drowning yourself in a lake.

O (*looking at Hamlet*): But... but I love him!

SW: There are plenty more idiots where that one came from, I assure you. What you need is a role model...

O: What is a role model?

SW: Oh, I forgot, that phrase doesn't come into fashion for another 300 years. Well, someone to look up to... someone to give you hope... someone to show you a new vision of life...

O: Like who?

SW: Well, how about Lady Raga?

Note: As we shall see, Lady Raga is a copy of Lady Gaga in her dress and mannerisms. Attendants bring forward Lady Raga props.

O: Who's Lady Raga?

SW: I can't explain. You need to experience it. Bring on the curtain! Let's have a little music.

WS (*alarmed*): Hey, what's going on? This isn't in my script!

Music plays. Attendants bring on a curtain to screen off Ophelia. She changes into her Lady Raga outfit while the music-intro is playing. Ophelia bursts out from behind the curtain in a skimpy white top, very tight shorts and a blonde wig and sings the blues song "Raga and her Baba:"

Raga and her Baba, we don't get along,
Raga and her Baba, this man he done me wrong.
Broke my heart in pieces and threw it on the floor,
Still I come back crying, begging him for more...
It's a crying shame... oooh yes it is... it's a crying shame...

Raga and her Baba, the man I love to hate,
Raga and her Baba, a passion that can't wait.
Broke my heart in pieces and threw it on the fire,
Still I come back crying, burning with desire...
It's a crying shame... oooh yes it is... it's a crying shame...

Song runs for approx. 1:45 min, then SW stops the music with a wave of her hand.

SW (*to Ophelia*): Stop! You've got the right idea,

     Anand Subhuti

sweetheart, but you're still focusing on Hamlet.
Take all the energy back and give it to yourself.
You are free to be you.

Ophelia: Free to be me?

*Music begins with a solo violin as background to
words that are half spoken, half sung.*

It's not the first time that you've said goodbye,
It's not the first time that you've made me cry,
But this time I have found a golden key,
Without you, I have freedom to be me...

*The music changes to a fast, driving beat. There's a
wild dance routine by Ophelia, with Shakespeare's
wife and the two Attendants doing a very hip
backing routine to support her.*

I'm free to be me, yeah, free to be me,
Free to be me, yeah, free to be me...

Free to say "No!" and free to say "Yes!"
Free turn on, say goodbye to the rest
Free to get high and dance all night long
Grab any guy and this is my song.

Free to say "Hi, I'm single and free,"
Free to say "You! You're coming with me!"
Free to say "Guy, are you looking at me?"
Free to say "Yeah, now, you're coming with me!"

I'm free to be me, yeah, free to be me,
Free to be me, yeah, free to be me...

*At the end, Ophelia and SW dance offstage, leaving
Hamlet alone with WS.*

WS (*Hamlet*): What are you smiling at?

H (*looking after Ophelia*): She's kinda cute, isn't she?

WS (*slowly and deliberately*): Young man, I am a genius in the use of English language and the word 'cute' does not appear in any of my plays. Ophelia is a tragic figure who is doomed to drown in a lake. Now, the big question is: how should YOU die?

H (*nervously*): Do I have to, Will?

WS: Of course, man. How can Hamlet be a tragedy if you don't die? (*calling out*) Where are the instruments of death?

An attendant brings a tray with a wine cup, a bottle of poison, an old flintlock pistol and two swords.

WS (*picking up the wine cup and bottle of poison*): Now, suppose the new king pours a glass of wine, sprinkles poison in it, then offers it to you to drink?

Hamlet reluctantly accepts the glass, then deliberately drops it.

H: Ooops! Sorry, I dropped it.

WS (*handing him the pistol*): Or, perhaps, in your despair, you put a pistol to your head and pull the trigger...

Hamlet does so and pulls the trigger but there is

just a 'click' and nothing happens.

H: Will, you forgot to load it!

WS: I have it! Hamlet must die in a sword fight. Come on man, take one of these and defend yourself.

H: (*to audience*): My god, do I really have to fight? Maybe I can scare him with my Clint Eastwood impersonation. (*to WS*) "Will, you've got to ask yourself one question: 'Do I feel lucky?' Well, do ya, punk?"

WS: You can't threaten me. I'm a Master Swordsman.

H: (*still imitating Clint Eastwood*): "Go ahead, make my day!"

WS: Where are you getting these cheap Hollywood lines from? Fight, man, fight!

H: (*to audience*) When all else fails... Arnold Schwarzenegger. (*to WS*) "Hasta la vista baby!"

Hamlet charges at WS, taking him by surprise. They fight. Shakespeare is losing and falls on the floor.

WS: Wait! Wait! I forgot. There must be treachery involved. (*to the attendant with the tray*) Give me that bottle of poison! (*drips it on his blade*) Your enemy has put poison on the tip of his sword. One small cut and all is lost. (*to Hamlet*) Look over there! (*he points behind him*).

Hamlet looks behind, Shakespeare makes a quick jab and cuts Hamlet's leg. Hamlet gasps and performs a long, overly-dramatic death, collapsing in a heap on the stage.

WS: That's much better!

Enter Queen Elizabeth.

E: Where is our playwright, Master Shakespeare?

WS (*kneeling immediately*): Here, your Majesty... your humble servant awaits your bidding.

E: We are interested in the progress of your a new play.

WS (*still kneeling*): Yes, your Majesty, it's coming along nicely.

E: What is this drama to be called?

WS: Hamlet, Prince of Denmark, your Majesty.

E: Indeed? We are curious as to how you intend this play to end... in *tragedy*, we trust?

WS: Oh yes, indeed, madam. (*Pointing to Hamlet's dead body*) All the main characters die.

E: Excellent. Our people must be continuously reminded that life is filled with melancholy, suffering and death.

Elizabeth exits. WS nudges Hamlet's body with his foot.

WS: Arise, O Corpse!

        Anand Subhuti

H (*looking up, surprised*): But I'm dead!

WS: No, no. That was just a temporary death to keep Her Majesty the Queen off my back (*helps him up*). Don't worry, you will die permanently later in the play.

H (*sarcastically*): Gee, thanks Will!

Hamlet limps offstage. Will goes back to his chair and starts writing. Enter Mrs Shakespeare. She walks to the front of the stage and addresses the audience directly.

SW (*to audience*): You seem like an intelligent group of people, so let me ask you a question. Don't you think it's odd that in the whole history of Western culture nobody knew anything about meditation?

WS (*standing up and joining his wife*): All those European geniuses...

SW: French Impressionist painters...

WS: Russian novelists...

SW: Italian sculptors...

WS: German composers...

Brief silence, as Will coughs and waits to be acknowledged.

SW: Oh yes, and not forgetting the English playwrights...

WS: Thank you, dear.

SW: And not one of them ever sat down, closed his eyes and meditated.

WS: They knew everything about the human ego...

SW: But they didn't know anything about dropping the ego.

WS: They knew how to be Somebody.

SW: But they had no idea how to be Nobody.

SW: Don't you think it's kind of odd?
Don't you think it's kind of strange?

WS: Such a funny situation
No one's heard of meditation.

SW: If you say the world is maya

WS: You will just be called a liar.

SW: If you point towards Nirvana

WS: They will say you've gone bananas.

SW If you tell them not to think

WS: They will send you to a shrink.

SW: If you ask them to be still

WS: They will offer you a pill.

SW: If you talk of inner vision

WS: They will think of television.

     Anand Subhuti

SW: If you sit silently alone

WS: Don't switch off your mobile phone.

SW: If you want to clear your head

WS: You can Google it instead.

SW: If you want true happiness

WS: Just send an SMS.

SW: If you want to raise your spirit

WS: Any shopping mall will do it.

SW: You can find out who you are

WS: At your local pub or bar.

SW: That's the story of the West,

WS: There's no time to stop and rest,

SW: Just to be...

WS: And let the rest...

SW: Disappear...

SW & WS: ...in emptiness...

WS and SW close their eyes for a moment, in silent meditation. Then they turn to face each other and give a Namaste. Mrs Shakespeare leaves the stage.

WS (*watching her go*): My wife's in love with Eastern

philosophy. Oh, it's interesting, I grant you, but what can you do with it? It's not going to pay the rent is it? It's not going to get me out of trouble with the queen. So, it's back to work for me...

He sits down and starts writing. Ophelia enters. Her 'Lady Raga' mood has disappeared and she is again hesitant and insecure.

O: Excuse me, Master Shakespeare.

WS *(irritated at being disturbed)*: Yes, what is it now?

O *(hesitantly)*: I... I want to change my character.

WS *(astonished)*: You... what?

O *(gathering courage)*: I want to change my character.

WS *(dismissively)*: No, no. That's not going to happen. The play is almost finished.

O *(kneels down by his chair and comes close with an appealing look)*: Please, sir! It's not much to ask, is it? I just want to live my own life. And you are such a clever genius, you can make anything possible.

WS *(noticing for the first time that she's beautiful and playing with her hair and cheeks)*: Hmm. You are a pretty little thing, aren't you? Listen, tomorrow my wife goes out of town to take care of her sick mother. Why don't you come to my house and we'll... talk about it... together... hmm?

O (*getting up and addressing the audience*): My god... this horny old goat is trying to seduce me! I've heard of the Hollywood casting couch... I've heard of the Bollywood casting couch... but I've never heard of an Elizabethan casting couch! Oh well, I guess it's always been the same. (*making herself look nice, as if she's giving in to his desire*) Right then...

O goes over to him seductively.

O: Oh Master Shakespeare
You're such a handsome man
And if you agree to help me
I'll give you what I can
(*She is all over him, caressing his face, etc*)
Would you like to taste my cherry?
It's so tender, it's so sweet!
Would you like to squeeze my plums
While I'm lying at your feet?
Shall I feed you some papaya
While we're lying on your bed?
Or would my lover rather have
A twisted nose instead?

(*Ophelia gives a hard yank to Will's nose*)

WS: Ow! You hurt me, you little bitch!

O: Well, you asked for it! You dirty old man!

WS: You will regret this young lady. You will die before this play is done. Your fate is sealed!

WS sits down with his play. Ophelia collapses weeping. Enter Mrs Shakespeare, who sits down beside her, gently takes her hand and comforts her with the following re-write of Charlene's song:

Hey lady, young lady, weeping at your life,
You want to be a princess and you want to be a wife.
I can see you long to be
His sweet beloved one
And I hope for you that your dreams come true,
Now your life has just begun.
I've searched and roamed many miles from home
Looking for that special one,
Enjoyed a fling with a foreign king
And we made love in the sun.
I met Will and I love him still
And yet I want to be free
I've been around the world
But I'd rather be with me

Hey lady, dear lady, you will have your day
From my heart I want to tell you
That everything's okay.
I can see your destiny
Reflected in your eyes
You won't be apart and your open heart
Can see through all the lies.

It's strange but true, and I'm telling you
That nothing ever lasts.
The future will be present
And the present will be past.
Now the hardest thing is to look within
And find the real me
I've been around the world
But I'd rather be with me.

Mrs Shakespeare holds Ophelia's hand.

　　　　　Anand Subhuti

Mrs S: Come along dear, we'll have a nice cup of tea.

They exit. Hamlet wanders on, sees the skull next to Will's chair, picks it up and looks at it.

H (*limping onstage*): Ow, that fake swordfight wasn't quite as 'fake' as I hoped. (*sees skull and picks it up*). But, on the other hand, it could have been worse! (*strikes a pose, holding up skull*) Alas, poor Yorick. You lost your head over a woman, didn't you? Well, that's not going to happen to me!

Hamlet tosses the rubber skull carelessly over his shoulder.

The character 'Nobody' comes onstage. He is dressed rather like an Indian sadhu, or holy man, but a little more jolly and friendly.

Nobody: Hi, how's it going?

Hamlet: Well, to be honest, I could use a few laughs. Who are you? What's your name?

N: Nobody.

H: Nobody? C'mon, you must be *somebody*.

N: Everybody tells me that: you *must* be *somebody*. But *anybody* can be somebody. And everybody *wants* to be somebody. Nobody wants to be *nobody*. Except me.

H: Can you say that again, slowly please?

N: Everybody says that, as well. *Nobody* understands.

H: But you *are* Nobody, so *you* must understand.

N: Anybody *could* understand, and I keep thinking one day somebody *will* understand. But believe me, nobody has any idea what Nobody is talking about.

H: Well, nobody's perfect.

N: Thank you, I agree!

H: No, that's not what I mean!

N: No worries. Nobody cares.

H: Okay, Mister Nobody, where are you from?

N: I'm from the Land of Not To Be.

H: I should have guessed.

N: Not to be, you see,
Is the only way to be.
Though you may disagree
Just listen carefully:
The more you think you've got,
The more you have to drop.
But, the more you find you're not
The more you've really got.

H: That's nonsense, don't you see?
Or would nobody agree?

Anand Subhuti

N: Nonsense it may be,
But would you agree
To check it out with me?

H: Well, okay... maybe.

N: Watch closely... you will see.

Enter Queen Elizabeth with attendants. It is time for the daily business in her court. First Attendant unrolls a scroll with a list of supplications from her people.

First Attendant: Your Majesty, the people of London have no bread to eat.

E: Let them eat cake.

First Attendant: Your Majesty, the people of York say your taxes are too high.

E: Let them work harder.

First Attendant: Your Majesty, the people of Lancaster wish you a happy birthday.

E (*slight smile*): Indeed? How touching. Let them make a statue of me, in gratitude.

The Royal group freezes, standing motionless.

N: Tell me, who is she?

H: Of course, 'tis Her Majesty

N (*reaching up towards her crown*): And if I remove her attire?

H (*alarmed*): Oh, I wouldn't do that, sire!

Nobody, not in the least worried, takes off her crown. The Queen reacts with a little gasp, as the crown is removed, but is still in trance. Nobody gives the crown to one of her Attendants.

E: Ah!

N: Who is this woman now, before whom you love to bow?

H: Well, no matter what it seems, she will still say she's the queen.

N: Without a crown with golden teeth?

H: Why certainly, 'tis her belief.

N: This belief, she wears it like a mask.

So this gives me another task (takes the mask off her face, gives it to Attendant).

H (*to the audience*): This Nobody is quite insane,
    She'll cut his head and eat his brains!

E (*bigger reaction but still in trance*): Oh! Who am I?

N: Your queen is stripped of power and glory
Who is she now in your Tudor story?

H: Why, looking simple, sad and sorry
This woman is just... ordinary.

Nobody (*very pleased*): Hamlet you have hit upon the truth

Anand Subhuti

And now the Queen will give you living proof
Now anything can happen, you will see
How 'not to be' makes everybody free...

Nobody pulls Hamlet to one side. Hip-hop dance music starts to play. Mrs Shakespeare and Ophelia come onstage in tight black leotards and start dancing like Beyonce, or similar style.

The Queen, under some kind of spell cast by Nobody, is enchanted and watches closely. At a certain point in the dance, the music stops.

E: What is this dancing that you do?
Can I learn to dance with you?

SW: Dear Madam, come and dance with us

Ophelia: We'll show you how to shake your ass.

Music starts again (from the beginning). The Queen joins in. The music continues for a while, then suddenly stops. The Queen looks shocked as she returns to her old self. Mrs Shakespeare and Ophelia look apprehensive.

SW: Uh-oh, I think we're in trouble.

Ophelia: Get ready to run.

Queen: What is happening in my court? These women are naked! Off with their heads! Off with their heads!

Mrs Shakespeare and Ophelia run off quickly, pursued by the Queen and Attendants.

Nobody (*to audience*): Of course, it doesn't always
work.
That Elizabeth is such a stupid jerk!
(*turns to Hamlet*)
Now, Hamlet, think what I have said,
Take off your mask and lose your head.

H (*confused*): I have no mask! It's not on me.

N (*laughs*): Oh yes, you have. You just can't see!

H: You've gone quite mad, I'll say good day!
And this Nobody can go his way.

N: Wait, spare a moment, let me ask,
This noble fellow with no mask,
This gloomy guy so filled with sadness
Who thinks that I am touched by madness.
Can you smile and sing and dance
If I give you half a chance?

H: Of course I can, if I so choose.
I've really nothing left to lose.

N: Then why be miserable and glum
When you can dance under the sun?

H: It isn't me who feels this way.
It's this bloody Bard who writes this play!

N: Come then, let's show this anti-fun guy
How they move it down in Mumbai!

*Music begins and Nobody leads Hamlet into a
popular Bollywood dance routine. Nobody does it
easily. Hamlet does his best to follow but soon
gives up.*

 Anand Subhuti

H: Stop! Stop! Enough! It's plain to see,
This Bollywood is not for me.

N: You're giving up because you're foreign?
Oh. Hamlet, this is really boring!

H: But I *can* dance, please have no fear... (*he puts
on a pair of dark glasses*)
Hi! My name's Psy... I'm from Korea!
Dressing classy, dancing cheesy
Gangnam Style is really easy!

*Music for Psy's Gangnam Style is played. Mrs
Shakespeare and Ophelia come onstage and join in.
Hamlet drags Will off his seat to dance. Everyone
joins in and dances like crazy. As the music ends,
Mrs Shakespeare and Ophelia exit. Will comes
center stage.*

WS: My god, what in the name of Her Majesty is
happening to my play? I will be thrown into the
Tower of London and left to rot forever!

*WS returns to his seat. Nobody and Hamlet are
left on stage.*

H: Okay Mr. Nobody, I'm beginning to see things
differently. But there's one thing I don't understand.
What would I gain from becoming a Not To Be?

N: Well, let's see... you wouldn't be the Prince of
Denmark any more... so you wouldn't be obsessed
with trying to avenge your father's death... so you
wouldn't spend all your time thinking "to be or
not to be"... *and* you wouldn't tell your beautiful
girlfriend to get lost.

H: Really?

N: Really.

H: How do I do it?

N: Ah, that can be a *little* challenging. Come with me.

They exit. Ophelia enters with SW.

O: Oh Mrs. Shakespeare, it was wonderful being Lady Raga. But I don't want to imitate anybody else. I want to be me.

SW: Really?

O: Really.

SW: Really... really?

O: Yes really. I just want to be myself.

SW: Well, that can be a *little* challenging. Come with me.

Enter Queen Elizabeth, with crown and mask.

E (*to WS*): Master Shakespeare, we are not pleased with the way this play is progressing.

WS: A thousand apologies Your Majesty.

E: We have not seen enough suffering and death to call it a tragedy.

WS (*thinking fast*): Fear not, Your Majesty. I am... er... I am planning a surprise. The play will seem to be heading in the direction of happiness, but, at the very end, I shall kill them all!

E: Very well. See that it is done, (*menacing*) or I promise you, thine head shall be impaled on a stake before the Tower of London.

WS: Oh no! I mean... oh yes, Your Majesty.

The Queen exits. Shakespeare goes to his chair. Attendants bring two chairs to the front centre of the stage. Nobody brings Hamlet to sit in one. SW brings Ophelia to sit in the other. Nobody stands behind Hamlet's chair. SW stands behind Ophelia's chair.

N: Not To Be requires an empty mind.

SW: A clear and quiet head.

N: We will represent your thoughts.

SW: When a thought enters your head, we will speak it for you.

N: In this way, you will become aware of your own thoughts.

SW: And most important, you will become aware of the silence *behind* your thoughts.

N: In that silence you will discover the Land of Not To Be.

SW: Close your eyes. Let us begin.

N and SW crouch down behind Hamlet and Ophelia. Each time a thought comes, they will stand erect and speak it.

N (*standing up*): This is easy... oh no, that's a thought! (*ducks down*)

SW (*standing up*): I just want to be myself... is this a thought?

N (*standing up and looking at SW*): Of course it is! (*ducks down*)

SW: But it's such a nice thought!

N: (*standing up again*): Nice thoughts... nasty thoughts... they all have to go! (*ducks down*).

SW (*shrugs*) Oh well... bye bye nice thought (*ducks down*).

N (*standing up*): I'm hungry! (*ducks down*).

SW (*standing up*): I'm thirsty (*ducks down*).

N (*standing up*): I'm restless (*ducks down*).

SW (*standing up*): I'm sad (*ducks down*).

N (*standing up*): To be or not to be?... oh, not again! (*ducks down*).

SW (*standing up*): I wonder if Hamlet still loves me? (*ducks down*).

N (*standing up*): I wonder what Ophelia looks like in the shower? (*as himself*) Now that's an interesting thought...

  Anand Subhuti

SW (*standing up, amused but firm*): Hey, keep your mind on the job, Mr. Not To Be!

N (laughing): Well, it's the first time he's actually expressed interest in her.

SW (*comes behind Hamlet and holds his head gently with her hands*): Isn't the male mind wonderful?

If it's not drowning women in lakes, it's gazing at them under the shower...

N: Wait... listen! Listen!

SW (*puzzled*): What do you hear?

N (*in wonder*): Nothing!

SW (*looking down at Hamlet and Ophelia*): Oh my god, they've done it. They've stopped thinking!

At the same moment, N and SW put a finger to their lips, then turn towards each other.

N & SW (*simultaneously*): Sssshhhhh!

They both stand with eyes closed, their hands in a mudra – buddha-like. But SW isn't very good at it and occasionally takes a quick peek at Nobody to see if he still has his eyes closed. Then she goes back to trying to meditate.

SW (*opening her eyes*): I wonder if I left my cooking pot on my stove.

N (*opening his eyes and rolling them upwards, while making an Italian gesture with his hands*): Oy vey! Now *you're* thinking!

SW (*rebuffing him*): Well, now *you're* thinking about me thinking. (*glances at Ophelia*)

N: Wait! She's going to say something.

Ophelia opens her eyes and looks lovingly at Hamlet and takes his hand. He opens his eyes and looks at her.

O: Hamlet, beloved, you still love me, don't you?

H: Yes, I do.

O: I knew it!

H: Shall we dance?

O: I'd love to!

They smile lovingly at each other.
Nobody and Mrs Shakespeare take away the chairs.
Hamlet and Ophelia dance to "There is a Country Far Away."

There is a country
Far away,
There is a land
Far away and lost.
There is a feeling
There is a healing
There is a country
A country of the heart.

Can this beauty that's there
Something so rare
Touch your heart, touch your heart, touch your heart?

Anand Subhuti

Can this love in the air
Something so rare
Ever let us part?

Mrs Shakespeare runs over and drags Will onto the dance floor. He is reluctant, but gives in and dances with his wife. Then all four dance together.

There is a secret in my soul
There is a deep mystery of love
There is a first time
There is a last time
There is a deep mystery of love

Can this beauty that's there
Something so rare
Touch your heart, touch your heart, touch your heart?
Can this love in the air...

WS breaks away from the other dancers and signals for the music to stop.

WS: Stop! Stop! All this romantic nonsense... it just won't do!

He shakes his head in frustration and goes back to his seat.

Hamlet (*to SW*): What happens now?

SW: Well, if you take my advice you'll both get out of Denmark as quickly as possible. It's such a miserable country. Why don't you go to India for the winter?

Ophelia: India! That sounds like a wonderful idea!

Hamlet: My god, but from Elizabethan England it will us take six months just to get there!

SW: No, no. I happen to know that Jet Airways is offering special flights from sixteenth century London. Look, (*removes tickets from her dress*) here are the tickets. Now run along both of you.

Will: Wait! Hold everything!

SW: Uh-oh.

Will (*walks forward a short way, then stops*): May I have a word with you... dear?

SW (*to Hamlet and Ophelia*): Just a minute. (*goes over to WS*). Yes, dear?

WS: Listen, beloved. I know you have good intentions and you want these young people to be happy, but if they don't die, I will. The Queen has threatened me with execution if this play does not end in tragedy.

SW: Ooooh, that nasty woman! But wait... I know... (*pulls more tickets out of her dress*) We'll all fly to India... right now, before she finds out.

WS: What? You want me to give up being the greatest playwright in England... just like that?

SW: Oh, I forgot. You haven't learned how Not To Be, have you?

WS (*indignant*): No, indeed. Nor will I ever do so. My name is going to be remembered for centuries and centuries.

SW (*takes him by the hand*): Will, love, come here (*takes him over to Hamlet and Ophelia*) Look at these beautiful young people. They've just discovered the joy of living. Do you want to take it away from them?

WS (*hesitating*): Well... er...

Queen Elizabeth enters with crown and mask. Two Attendants follow her, carrying swords.

E: Off with their heads!

WS (*bowing*): Your Majesty.

E: Why are these young people not yet dying or dead?

WS: Soon, soon, Your Majesty. I'm just about to kill them.

E: Do it now. I command it! Off with their heads!

WS: Yes, Your Majesty. I'm sorry, both of you. A thousand pardons, but it is your destiny to die in my play.

Enter Nobody, disguised as Death, with black hood and skull face.

N (*hollow voice*): Your time has come, Your Majesty.

E (*shrieks in fright*): Eeeek! Oh god! Who are you, pray?

N: I am the Angel of Death. And it is your time to die!

E (*clutches her heart*): Ah, it is true! (*staggers forward a little*). My heart is giving out! (*theatrically brushes her forehead with her hand*) It is my time! (*sinks to her knees*) Farewell, cruel world! Farewell! I die! I die! I die!

Elizabeth staggers off, supported by her Attendants.

Nobody takes off his death mask.

N: That was pretty good acting, eh Will?

WS: Well, obviously the queen thought so. She died of fright. Who are you?

N: I'll tell you later. But first, we must find a way to end this play properly.

SW, Ophelia, Hamlet (*together*): A happy ending!

WS (*stubbornly*): No. I refuse to write a happy ending.

N: But why?

WS: It's so ordinary, so predictable. Look at this sophisticated audience. You can't expect them to take me seriously as a playwright if I write a happy ending.

SW (*folding her arms*): Well, we refuse to take part in a tragic ending.

H and O (*also folding their arms*): Right!

N: I know. How about a thriller?

SW: A thrilling ending, yes!

Anand Subhuti

WS: But I've never ever written a thriller.

N: It's easy. Listen, Will... (he whispers in WS's ear).

WS (*smiling*): Okay. I'll try it. Take your places everyone!

Lights down. Music starts from Michael Jackson's "Thriller." WS dances like Michael Jackson and lip-sychs the words, while the rest are dancing as zombies.

WS (*lip-synching*): "It's close to midnight and something evil's lurking in the dark..."

The song continues for a couple of minutes, including two choruses of "It's Just a Thriller, Thriller Night..." Then, suddenly, the music is interrupted by a Royal fanfare of trumpets. Queen Elizabeth comes on to the stage, followed by Attendants. Everyone kneels down and is worried.

E:
One moment. Please don't be afraid
Of being hurt by this old maid.
If I may choose twixt life and death
I'd really rather keep my breath.
So let me join you in your gladness
And say goodbye to royal sadness.

SW (*taking Elizabeth warmly by the arm*):
Your Majesty, I'm glad to see
That, deep inside, you're just like me!

WS (*to N*):
So tell me, Master Nobody
Where is this Land of Not To Be?

N:
Well, if you look beyond your mind
You'll find it's been there all the time.
But meditation is more fun
If to India you come!

E:
India! Oh yes, that's hip!
If my old bones can make the trip.
I think I'll go to Dharamshala
And hang out with the Dalai Lama.

Attendants (*still wanting to please her*):
Oh yes, Your Majesty, it's true
Can we come along with you?

E (*to her Attendants*):
I think it's time for you to see
You really don't belong to me.
Nobody (*to Attendants*):
Find a path that suits *you* best,
And give this 'royal' thing a rest!

Mrs Shakespeare:
Yoga is what I love best.
And so I'll go to Rishikesh.
Sitting by the Ganges stream
Enjoying yoga - that's my dream!
I'll practice my asanas daily
Standing on my head... well, maybe.

Anand Subhuti

Attendants:
Oh yes we're good at yoga, too,
Perhaps we'll come along with you.

Mrs Shakespeare:
Find a method of your own
Don't just follow... stand alone.

Hamlet (*to Ophelia*):
I'm sure we'll get enlightened sooner
If we meditate in Pune.

Ophelia (*worried*):
But isn't that the 'free love' ashram?
Will I lose my love, my passion?

Attendants:
Don't worry, dear, we'll come with you
And sing and dance the whole night through!

Hamlet (*taking Ophelia's hand and taking her away from the Attendants*):
That won't be necessary, good fellows.
We can celebrate by ourselves.
We'll go to Pune as a pair
A challenge will await us there.

Ophelia (*no longer afraid, but courageous*):
Let's see if we can both be free
And true lovers still shall be.

Will:
All my life I've been a playwright
Finding words to make you say right.
So maybe I should shut up now
And silently meditate somehow.
I'll find a monastery in Ladakh

And take the pressure off my back.

1st Attendant:
Let's join the Bard in silence deep
2nd Attendant:
If it doesn't make us go to sleep.

Nobody (*to Attendants*):
Now stop this nonsense, both of you
Find something specially meant for you!

1st Attendant:
Okay, we'll walk the Himalayan hills
From end to end in search of thrills.
2nd Attendant:
We'll trek from Kathamanadu to Kulu
And touch the feet of every guru.

Nobody:
Now I can say goodbye in style,
Let me vanish for a while.
Nobody was never here,
It's time for me to disappear.
If you wish, you can find me
In the Land of Not To Be.

Will:
Meet we all, here, in one year
There'll be so much for us to hear.
I'll write a new play, make amends,
Called Shakespeare the Meditator And His Friends.

Everyone:

Another drama for you to see,
Another story ends happily
In meditation, in ecstasy,

　　　　　　Anand Subhuti

In the Land of Not to Be.
Another drama to make you smile,
Another story performed in style
We'll see you later, in a while,
In the Land of Not to Be.

Heroes, zeroes, kings and queens
Come to India it seems.
Cleopatra longs to be
In Rishikesh with Anthony,
Juliet and Romeo
Left for Pune long ago.
Let your heart be open wide
Close your eyes and go inside.
There is more for you and me
In the Land of Not to Be.

Another drama for you to see,
Another story ends happily...

The End

www.ingramcontent.com/pod-product-compliance
Lightning Source LLC
Chambersburg PA
CBHW020105310726

48970CB00002B/488